A BOY IS NOT A BIRD

A BOY IS NOT A BIRD

Edeet Ravel

GROUNDWOOD BOOKS
HOUSE OF ANANSI PRESS
TORONTO / BERKELEY

Groundwood Books / House of Anansi Press
groundwoodbooks.com

We gratefully acknowledge for their financial support of our publishing
program the Canada Council for the Arts, the Ontario Arts Council and
the Government of Canada.

 Canada Council **Conseil des Arts**
for the Arts **du Canada**

 ONTARIO ARTS COUNCIL
CONSEIL DES ARTS DE L'ONTARIO
an Ontario government agency
un organisme du gouvernement de l'Ontario

With the participation of the Government of Canada
Avec la participation du gouvernement du Canada | Canadä

Library and Archives Canada Cataloguing in Publication
Title: A boy is not a bird / Edeet Ravel.
Names: Ravel, Edeet, author.
Identifiers: Canadiana (print) 20190043857 | Canadiana (ebook) 20190043873 |
ISBN 9781773061740 (hardcover) | ISBN 9781773061757 (EPUB) |
ISBN 9781773061764 (Kindle)
Classification: LCC PS8585.A8715 B69 2019 | DDC jC813/.54—dc23

Illustrations by Pam Comeau
Map by Mary Rostad
Cover photo courtesy of Nahum Halpern
Design by Michael Solomon

MIX
Paper from
responsible sources
FSC® C016245

For Nahum, Gina, Tammy and Dafna
and for my darling Ivy
who is all new

ONE
MINUS A HOUSE

1940
SUMMER

1

Something Is Wrong

My best friend Max and I are playing a game called Life and Death on the High Seas. Max came up with both the game and the name. He gets all the good ideas. I'm more of a go-along type of guy.

It's our summer holidays. In three weeks we'll be back in school, which means homework, teachers (including, unfortunately, Mrs. Bubu), waking up early, and our entire lives charted out like a multiplication table.

For now, though, we're as free as the wind. Max jumps up on the big crate we've been sitting on. The crate is our ship. We're headed for Montreal, Canada, where my relatives live.

"Hold on to the mast, hold on to the mast!" Max cries out, wobbling from side to side. His round glasses flash and flicker in the sun and his orange-red hair glows as if it's on fire.

"The waves are getting higher and higher," I shout back. "Grab a raft before we drown!"

"Watch out for pirates!"

"Boys, boys," a voice calls from behind us.

It's Max's mother, standing in the middle of the stormy sea. Except that it's not the sea, of course. It's Max's front garden. The chickens are pecking at the ground, looking for seeds. Near the shed, Max's older brother Michael is chopping wood.

"You'd better head on home, Natt," Max's mother says. She always speaks in a soft voice — so soft that her friends call her Kitten. But she sounds a little wild suddenly, and there's a strange look in her eyes, as if she's trying to hide something. "Your mother will be worrying."

I'm confused. Why would Mama worry? She knows where I am.

But I take the hint. Max's mother wants me to leave.

Maybe there's a medical emergency somewhere, and Max's dad needs him. Max's father is a doctor, and when he pays a visit to a poor person who has small children, he asks Max to come along and keep an eye on the kids while he attends to the patient.

"Only if it's a broken arm or something like that," Max said with his usual wide grin, when he first told me about these trips. "Not if it's that bug that turns you into a werewolf. The first symptom is sudden drooling."

Max may be on the small side, but he does a pretty convincing imitation of a drooling lupine monster.

I remember my manners and thank Max's mother for having me. I even give a little bow, because it usually makes her laugh.

But today, Mrs. Zwecker barely notices.

"Be careful — it's a full moon tonight!" Max calls out as I let myself through the gate.

I would have liked to spend more time with Max, but there are plenty of fun things to do at home. As a reward for my good grades last year, my parents bought me a magnifying glass, a telescope and a kaleidoscope. I can now spend hours in my room looking at small things getting bigger, faraway things getting nearer, and geometric shapes expanding and contracting.

As well as being a go-along type of boy, I'm also the stay-at-home type. I'm not crazy about sports, partly because I have asthma, and partly because I'm a bit on the chubby side. According to my mother, some kids don't lose their childhood chubbiness until they're twelve. One year to go.

Max loves sports. You wouldn't think such a tiny kid could kick so hard or run so fast, but it's as if he's got invisible wings on his boots when he goes after that soccer ball.

As I walk home, I entertain myself with a game I invented — the only game I've thought of myself, without Max. I try to think of a word that's different in all the languages I know.

My first and best language is German. That's what I speak at home and with Max.

Our town, Zastavna, has a large Ukrainian population, so everyone who lives here is fluent in Ukrainian. Ukrainian has some *very* bad words. Max's brothers told him what those words mean and Max told me. It's useful to have a friend with older brothers.

Third language: Romanian. That's what they teach us in school. We're not really allowed to speak German to each other at school, but we do anyhow.

My fourth language is Hebrew. Ordinary school begins after lunch, but in the mornings Max and I attend Hebrew classes in Mr. Elias's house.

Finally, there's Yiddish, which some Jews speak at home. It's similar to German but has a mind of its own. Yiddish is famous for its sayings —

If you don't open your mouth, a fly won't get in.
Sleep faster, we need the pillows.
What will happen to the sheep if the wolf is the judge?

That's five languages swirling around in my head! Sometimes I don't know which language I'm speaking until someone reminds me.

My game might sound easy, but it isn't. Take the word for mother. Romanian, Ukrainian and Hebrew are all different, but German and Yiddish, *Mutter*, are the same.

I'm concentrating on my game and kicking a pebble down the road when suddenly I notice that something is wrong.

It's the quiet.

In beautiful weather like this, with the sun shining in a cloudless blue sky, you'd expect to see kids playing, grown-ups rushing around and cart drivers shouting at everyone to move out of the way of the horses.

But the streets are completely deserted.

I almost stop breathing.

What if the Iron Guard are on their way here?

The entire town is terrified of the Iron Guard. They're a group of ferocious, bloodthirsty men who wear green jackets and hate everyone. Mr. Elias calls them fascists. Max calls them "potato slime in human form."

They usually start off with a march or parade, but that part doesn't last long. At some point they go berserk. They break into homes and businesses and sometimes they kill the people inside. They especially hate Jews, but luckily we look like everyone else, so unless there's someone from our town marching with them, they don't know who we are.

I've never actually seen them, because my parents and I always hide behind bags of grain in my father's warehouse when we hear them coming. We have a special hiding place, like a little fort, with books to keep us happy. We don't have to worry about the sound of pages turning. The Iron Guard make so much noise that they can't hear anyone else.

And the bags of grain are too heavy for them to lift.

But not everyone has a fort. My friend Zigi had a close call. They smashed the windows of his parents' bakery and threw the cakes and bread on the floor. They would have killed Zigi and his parents while they were at it, but the three of them managed to escape to a church in the nick of time.

The Iron Guard never kill anyone in a church. I guess they think God can't see them on the street.

I look around for the nearest steeple. I'm three or four minutes away, if I make a dash for it.

Instead, I run home as fast as I can.

Being alone in a church is spooky, and what if the door is locked?

2

Alien Radio

I run as if a fire-breathing demon is chasing me. By the time I reach our house my chest hurts and I'm wheezing. I hurry along the veranda that circles our house and enter the kitchen from the back.

No one is there.

Normally at this hour my mother and Lana, our housemaid, are busy preparing supper. But the table hasn't even been set.

What if the Iron Guard marched in and killed everyone in the house? My head begins to swim, and I grab at the stove tiles to steady myself.

"Natt? Is that you?"

As soon as I hear my mother's voice, I feel like an idiot. She's in another room, that's all.

Why am I such a baby?

"Darling boy!" she exclaims as she comes into the kitchen. "You're as pale as a ghost."

"It's my asthma … I was … running."

"Why were you in such a hurry?" she asks.

I sink into a chair. I'm not going to tell her that I thought she and Papa and Lana had been murdered. I don't want to lie, but I don't want to tell the truth either, so the best thing is to say nothing.

But my mother, as always, reads my mind. She smiles. "Did something scare you? What was it? Hmm … let me guess. A snarling dog? A great big bear?"

My mother hasn't noticed that I'm no longer two years old. Maybe her jokes were funny back then, but that was a long, long time ago.

"I know! A goblin with purple ears."

"There was no one on the street," I say, trying to sound nonchalant. "I thought the Iron Guard was coming."

She shakes her head. "Poor Natt. No, it's nothing like that."

I truly hate being a soft egg, as we say in German. A soft egg is a person who is not exactly famous for courage and daring. Max and I call ourselves the Two Musketeers, and our Musketeer names are Maximus and Natius. But we both know I'm not much of a Musketeer.

Max is the opposite of me. Nothing frightens him — whether it's creaks at night or bats in the attic. Even Mrs. Bubu, who would probably join the Iron Guard if they took women, doesn't frighten him.

Max just turns scary things into a joke. If we had to fight an enemy, he wouldn't hesitate for a second. He may be on the short side, he may have glasses, but he'd draw his sword out of its scabbard and lunge!

My eyes fall on several pairs of boots lined up by the front door. We have guests! At least ten, judging by the boots. But where are they? And why can't I hear them?

Again, my mother reads my mind. "Some friends have dropped by because we have a good radio, and they want to hear about some important events that are happening in the world."

Some important events that are happening in the world! This is why I usually have to get the low-down from Max. My mother is convinced that I'm too young to understand big words or complicated ideas.

It makes sense, though, that people would come to our house to listen to the radio. Our town didn't have electricity until three years ago, and lots of people still aren't connected to the power poles.

Max says it's because we live in a "godforsaken backwater, light years away from civilization." He likes to joke about our small town.

But we're not really out in the sticks. Even by horse and cart, we're only a few hours from Czernowitz, which is the biggest city in all of Bukovina and one of the most famous cities in Eastern Europe.

I can hear the low murmur of the radio now. Odd that it sounds so distant. Our radio is in the living room and normally I'd hear it in the kitchen, if it was on.

My mother says, "Aunt Dora brought cinnamon cookies. You can have one if you promise it won't spoil your appetite. Just this once, because supper is going to be late."

There she goes again. There's something huge going on in the world, and my mother seems to think that all I'm interested in is a cookie. Though to tell the truth, I'm kind of starving. On top of that, my aunt is famous for her baking.

My mother hurries back to the visitors.

I sit alone at the table and munch on the delicious cookie. I have to stay put until I finish. That's a rule in our house. No eating anywhere other than the kitchen. We don't want mice seeking their fortune in other rooms.

It's strangely quiet in the house, considering that we have guests.

I'm used to a lot of hustle and bustle at home. My father has a team of men who help him with his grain business, and they're in and out of the house all the time. My favorite is Olek, who has a brown-and-white sheepdog called Zoomie. When I stand on a stepladder so I can reach the pears dangling from the tree in our garden, Zoomie thinks it's a contest to see who's taller and she springs up from the ground like a jack-in-the-box. She's so hilarious! I swear she bounces five feet in the air.

And there's our housemaid Lana, who's sixteen and lives with us. Where is she?

I forget to brush the crumbs off my shorts before standing up, and they scatter on the floor as I head for the living room. Oh, well. With a bit of luck, my mother will be too preoccupied with *important world events* to notice.

I trot down the narrow hallway on my imaginary Musketeer's horse, Lightning III.

But the living room is empty. No guests. And no radio.

I listen again. The rumble of the radio seems to be coming from my parents' bedroom.

Impossible! My mother would never allow strangers in her bedroom. True, the reception is better there, but my mother says it's "indecorous" to let visitors into the private section of the house.

I tug at my reins and follow the sound. The door to my parents' bedroom is half-open. I dismount and peek inside.

At least twenty faces turn to look at me. The guests are crammed into every corner, and they're so still they could be posing for a painting.

And my mother seems perfectly fine with all these guests in the bedroom! The news must be even more earth-shaking than I'd imagined.

A voice comes crackling through the radio on the bedside table. It's the BBC, broadcasting in German. That's what we mostly listen to, when we can, but suddenly the radio's two knobs look like the eyes of an alien from Mars.

Our lawyer, Mr. Bruno Jacobson, is here, of course. He lives in a separate apartment at the side of our house. He doesn't have a single hair on his head, and Max and I call him Bruno the Bald. He's got his notebook with him and he's taking notes with a tiny pencil.

Dr. Shiff, the dentist from across the street, is holding his chin in both hands, as if he's the one with a toothache. I'm friends with his daughter, Lucy, who always smells good because her uncle has a cosmetics factory in Budapest and he sends her perfumed soap. Lucy's mother is in a sanatorium, and Lucy's an only child like me, so she often drops by after supper to play checkers and card games. But for some reason she stayed home today.

Lana stands near the bureau with her arms folded. She's the only one who smiles when she sees me.

To my surprise, I see one of my teachers from school. His wife is by his side, holding a sleeping baby in her arms. He hasn't noticed me. I'm glad. He raps our knuckles and Max keeps hoping he'll sit on a thumbtack.

My violin teacher, Mr. Drabik, is looking right at me but he's taken off his glasses and doesn't see me. His wife holds on to his arm. She calls me Mr. Moonlight because I always ask her to play Beethoven's "Moonlight Sonata" on the piano. If I owned that record I'd listen to it on my aunt's gramophone every spare minute I had.

The Drabiks have a daughter, Irena, who lives in Czernowitz, where she's studying to be a teacher. Mrs. Drabik lets me and Max borrow Irena's books. She has a whole set of German translations with loads of pictures: *Robinson Crusoe, The Legends of King Arthur, Dr. Jekyll and Mr. Hyde* ...

My parents say I'm a born bookworm, but Max reads even more than I do. So far, our favorites are *Kidnapped* and *Treasure Island*. "Fifteen men on the dead man's chest — Yo-ho-ho, and a bottle of rum!"

3

Too Late to Escape

It isn't until the guests have left that my father explains, over the supper table, what's happening.

Bruno the Bald, still clutching his notebook, joins us for the meal, even though he has a kitchen of his own and usually prefers to eat by himself, or with his very tall friend Andreas. We like to make up stories about Bruno the Bald and Andreas the Tall. Sometimes they're heroes who help Natius and Maximus, and sometimes they're pranksters who play tricks on us.

Lana joins us once she's finished serving the soup. She's part of the family as far as I'm concerned. I like to watch her peel potatoes or draw water from the well or scrub our clothes in a big metal basin. I especially like helping when she hangs sheets on the clothesline. She asks me to hold one corner of the sheet while she pegs the other corner to the line. I keep wanting to touch her blonde braids, but I don't dare.

Lana always chats as she works. She tells me that one day she's going to move to the United States and live in a big mansion and wear long silk gloves. She says her wedding cake will be three feet high and decorated with two thousand pink roses made of sugar. I nod my head as if I believe every word.

And maybe she will marry a millionaire one day. I don't know if she's named after Lana Turner, who starred in a movie I saw last year, but she's just as beautiful.

Papa turns to me and says, "Well, my little *Schild-kröte.*" That's his pet name for me — turtle — because sometimes I get so wrapped up in a book that he imagines I'm hiding inside it, especially when the book is very big, like the atlas.

"You must be wondering what this is all about," he continues.

Do I really want to know? I'm not sure, so I mumble, "Ummm" — which is what I do when I can't decide what to say.

"Last summer, Hitler signed a pact with Stalin, the leader of Russia. You probably remember everyone talking about it."

I nod. My parents don't discuss the news with me, but Max's sisters keep him up to date on world events. To be honest, all that political jibber-jabber doesn't interest me much. I don't want to think about the war, and my parents don't want me to think about it, either. A few times we've had refugees stay with us for several days — mostly Jews from Germany or

Poland. The German army has been invading countries for the past year, and they definitely have it in for the Jews.

My mother didn't let the refugees talk about the war in front of me, but I picked up bits and pieces. Midnight escapes, close calls, secret enemies. Like something out of an adventure book.

"As a result," my father explains, "Russia is now taking over this part of the country. So in a few days you'll be learning Russian, with all new teachers. The good news is that the Iron Guard won't be bothering us anymore."

Russian? That makes language number six. Now my language game will be even harder.

"In Russian, you are a *malchik*," he says. "Can you guess what that is?"

"Boy!" I exclaim. The last part, *chik*, is the same as Ukrainian.

"Excellent," my father says. "It's a beautiful language. Russia has some of the world's greatest writers. Chekhov, Tolstoy, Dostoevsky ..."

Well, all this sounds like good news. So why is everyone on edge?

My mother, as usual, guesses what I'm thinking. It's mostly annoying, but it can be convenient in emergencies.

"Yes," she says, "we're concerned. The change

means we don't know what the future holds. But then we never know the future in this life."

Lana, who's serving the mashed potatoes, winks at me. She's thinking about her American millionaire.

"It's my fault," my mother adds with a sigh. "We could have been safe and sound in Montreal by now."

When I was five, my parents decided to move to Canada. Our relatives in Montreal described the city in their letters, and I used to go to bed imagining the skyscrapers, the motor cars, the big stores — and the huge mountain in the middle of the city. A million people, all in one place!

I didn't worry about missing Max back then, because I didn't know him yet.

Each week my father would go to the city and run from office to office, lining up for hours at each one, trying to get the necessary documents.

At last he had everything he needed.

But after all that, my mother changed her mind.

"How can I leave my friends and family?" she asked, turning the palms of her hands face up, as if an answer might drop down from the sky. "How can I tear myself away from this beautiful house and our precious garden? We'd have to live in a tiny apartment and learn a whole new language. And how would we make a living?"

I could tell Montreal scared her. Not because it's a big city. Vienna, where she grew up, is twice the size of Montreal. She likes to tell us about the museums and concert halls of Vienna, and about the cafés on Praterstrasse where her father played chess with his friends.

Our relatives in Montreal had promised to look after us. *Montreal is so safe that people go to bed at night without locking their doors,* they wrote in their letters.

But my mother was afraid of being lonely in such a far-off place.

Now, six years later, it's too late.

Everyone wants to leave now. But it's no longer possible, with or without papers.

I go to bed wondering what the new Russian teachers will be like. I'm glad Max will be there with me. His desk is right next to mine. As long as it's the two of us against the world, I'm not afraid. I only have to catch a glimpse of his ear-to-ear grin and rolling eyes, and I know that the minute we're alone, he'll do imitations of all the adults and send me into hysterics.

As I draw the blanket up to my chin, a thought occurs to me — the kind of thought Max calls a Sudden Flash of Genius. *All new teachers means an end to Mrs. Bubu! She'll be gone forever!!*

I let out a great sigh of joy. Everyone is going to be over the moon. One look from Mrs. Bubu and you feel you should probably offer to die, just to save time.

4

A Dog Barking at Birds

It's been four days since we heard the big news about Russia on the radio. My parents tune in to the BBC as often as possible and everyone asks them for reports on the latest news.

Nothing much has happened, in fact, but this morning, when I come into the kitchen for breakfast, the first thing I see is a carved metal box on the table, next to the salt and pepper shakers.

My father places his hand on the box and says, "Natt, we're going to let you in on a grown-up secret, because you're such a clever and mature boy now."

I sit up in my chair and do my best to look clever and mature.

He lifts the lid of the box. There are gold coins inside! Real gold, like in *Treasure Island*. Under the coins lie a few American dollar bills.

"Tonight, when it gets dark, we're going to bury this box behind the barn. It will be our secret. Only Aunt Dora and Uncle Isaac will know where the treasure is hidden. We're also going to hide a diamond ring and some other precious coins and jewels inside the lining of Mama's coat. It's good to have these things for emergencies."

Emergencies? What kind of emergencies? I don't like the sound of this at all.

My mother sees me not liking the sound of it.

She reaches over and ruffles my hair. I force myself not to flinch or pull away. Luckily, it's a short ruffle.

"When countries are fighting," she says, "there can be a lot of confusion. You can't predict from one day to the next what will happen. Imagine a flock of birds sitting together quietly on a haystack, enjoying the fine weather. A dog runs up to them and begins to bark, and with a big squawk and a tangle of wings they fly away, up, up to the sky, in different directions. The war is the barking dog. But the birds will eventually come together again, and everything will return to the way it was before."

My father nods. "War is when you get a chance to be a hero. Because every day that you get through it, you've done something heroic."

This sounds even worse.

"Get through it how?" I ask.

"Get through whatever comes your way," my father says, flinging his arm as if he were brushing away some pesky flies. "And you, Natt," he continues, "are definitely hero material. No matter what, you will always be courageous, keeping in mind that the birds, as Mama says, will find their way back after the war."

Courageous! My father must know I'm afraid of the dark, of tree branches at night, of creatures that don't even exist. I'm scared of strict teachers and big kids who pick on little kids. Once I almost had a heart attack when an owl came swooping out of a tree and seemed to be coming for my hat. I ran for my life.

Most embarrassing of all, as a treat for my fourth birthday, my mother took me to the city to see a movie, and when a train on the screen came charging at us, and the audience gasped, I began to scream. What a dope! My mother had to carry me out of the cinema and it took me half an hour to calm down. Luckily she didn't tell anyone outside the family. What would Lana think?

All of a sudden, we hear a huge rumbling that sounds like distant thunder, followed by loud voices and commotion. I jump out of my chair and clutch my father's arm. That's exactly what I'm talking about. Such a soft egg!

I quickly let go of my father and try to look unimpressed. In fact there's something friendly about the sound outside. We hurry to the front door and peek out.

A great big choir is coming our way. Russian soldiers are marching through the streets singing a loud, cheerful song. It's the kind of song that makes you want to join in.

"They have beautiful voices," my mother says hopefully. An army that sounds like a performing choir can't possibly be up to no good.

"The Russians are very musical," my father agrees. "They love to sing."

There are tanks, too, rolling along on their chains, and three or four trucks.

I've never seen anything like this. Everyone comes out to watch the parade. The soldiers seem to be in a good mood, and they don't look dangerous. They're nothing like the Iron Guard.

"What are they singing?" I ask my father.

He translates some of the words for me:

We were marching in the scorching heat
For our teacher, our leader!
We've been sent to fight for Comrade Stalin!

Comrade means buddy or pal in German: *Kamerad*.

"That's a funny word to use for a leader," I say. Buddy Stalin!

My father nods. "In Russia, the word *comrade* means that we're all brothers and sisters, and no one is better than anyone else. The French used it that way first, during the French Revolution."

Well, I know all about the French Revolution, when the people rose up against the king. I've read *Beware the Guillotine!*

I also know about the Russian Revolution, which took place when my father was a teenager. But in Russia, a few months after they got rid of Tsar Nicholas II, the Communists took over.

You don't have to be Russian to be a Communist. We even have a few secret Communists in our town, or at least that's the rumor. I don't really understand the difference between the Communists, the Socialists, the Nationalists … it's all very confusing. My parents don't like to talk to me about current events. "Words can get you into hot water," my father always reminds me. "Think before you speak."

The soldiers stop marching before they reach our house. They begin chatting with the townspeople. Some families hand them flowers and offer them food or mugs of tea.

If the soldiers see a watch, they ask for it, and the person has no choice but to hand it over. Bad luck for Bruno the Bald, who always wears a pocket watch with the gold chain showing. He has to pull the watch out of his pocket and give it to a Russian soldier. He's practically in tears. The watch belonged to his father.

The soldiers are excited about their new watches. The bigger the watch, the more excited they are.

I notice that quite a few of the soldiers have torn boots, with their toes poking out between the flaps. I feel a little sorry for them, even if they did take all those watches.

Across the street, I see my friend Lucy, and I call out to her in German. She answers me in Yiddish.

There's an officer sitting on a tank nearby, and when he hears us, he calls us over — in Yiddish! He's a Jew! A Russian soldier who is also Jewish. I'm feeling better by the minute.

A dozen people immediately surround the officer and hurl a storm of questions at him. *What's going to happen? What do the Russians have in mind? Will the men be called up to join the army?*

The officer smiles as he answers our questions in Yiddish. He refers to Stalin as *Hahver*, friend.

"Everything will be wonderful," he assures us. "We are all Soviet citizens now, and *Hahver* Stalin will take good care of us."

5

Comrade Martha and Comrade Minsky

The holidays are over! We're back in school. The same building, but all new rules. And new teachers, too.

A skinny man walks into our classroom. His clothes are too big on him, and he has sad, anxious eyes that make me think of a rabbit. He looks scared of us, scared of the classroom, scared of his own shadow.

We all start giggling. What a relief! We don't have to be scared of a teacher who's scared of us.

Right behind our new teacher there's a poster I've never seen before. It shows a man with a friendly moustache holding a cute little kid in his arms. The kid has a flag in one hand and white flowers in the other.

I'm excited to be in a mixed class for the first time. Until now, girls and boys were in different classrooms.

It's more fun this way. In fact, Lucy's desk is right next to mine, which means I'm sitting between my two best friends. Lucy turns to smile at me. I smile back and inhale deeply. Now I can enjoy the sweet smell of lavender soap all day long.

Our new teacher leans against the wall without saying a word. Every few seconds he glances at the door as if he's expecting someone to come and rescue him.

And that's what happens. The door opens and in marches a woman who is the exact opposite of the timid man. She looks strong and healthy and sturdy. She's wearing a pretty green-and-white dress and there's a small picnic basket on her arm.

All our teachers so far have been either strict and mean or (in rare cases) strict and nice. But this woman acts as if she's an older sister who adores us. Her smile is so wide it makes her eyes shine.

"Hello," she says in Ukrainian. "*Dobroye utro!* That's *good morning* in Russian. I'm Comrade Martha. Welcome to your new school, where we are going to learn to be good citizens so we can do our duty and serve our leader."

She turns to the poster of the man with the moustache, and her eyes get even shinier.

"This is our great leader and father, Comrade Stalin, and he has a little present for you."

She lifts the lid of her wicker basket and hands out candy canes! This is definitely our lucky day.

More good news follows.

"There is absolutely no hitting of children allowed

in this school. Our glorious leader loves children. You are our future. And I know you all want to be Pioneers. That is our goal, to be Pioneers. And whoever passes all the requirements and becomes a Pioneer will be rewarded and will get the chance to do lots of fun things. Whoever misbehaves loses that chance and will be very sad, because no one will want to be friends with that little boy or girl."

We look at each other with astonishment. The worst part of school is rulers on hands or pulling of ears (Mrs. Bubu's area of expertise). Or even, in some cases, the strap.

Max reaches over and squeezes my arm.

"We will no longer have morning shift and afternoon shift. Everyone will study together, from eight in the morning to mid-afternoon, Sunday to Friday, with Saturdays off. Sundays are half-days and will be devoted to fun games and revolutionary activities."

We'll have to let Mr. Elias know. Our Hebrew class will have to move to after school.

"And I'm afraid you all have to repeat grade four," Comrade Martha adds.

When we hear this, we're speechless. Did we all fail? How is that possible?

A girl in the corner begins to sob. It's Mariana, the smallest girl in the class. She's nearly always barefoot, unless it's actually snowing, and she cries at the drop of a hat.

Comrade Martha goes over to Mariana and lifts her in her arms. She gives her a kiss and says, "It's only because you will be learning in Ukrainian and Russian now."

"But I already know Ukrainian," Mariana sniffles, and everyone laughs, including Comrade Martha.

"Don't worry, you will learn all new things. Comrade Stalin wants you to be happy. And we are going to find you a pair of shoes, dear. Are you happy?" she asks.

Mariana nods, and Comrade Martha lowers her gently back into her chair. Then she joins the scared little man at the front of the classroom and places her arm around his shoulder.

"This, my young friends, is Comrade Minsky. He is going to teach you all your subjects, including Russian. You are very, very lucky, because Comrade Minsky is a professor who taught at a famous Moscow university. And now here he is, coming all this way to teach you! I want you all to say, *Bolshoe spacibo,* Comrade Minsky, for coming to teach us."

We repeat the words after her. Comrade Minsky tries to smile, but the smile is so crooked it reminds me of a twig mouth on a snowman.

"There will be many treats in your future, if you work hard," Comrade Martha promises. "And when you are Pioneers, you will get a red kerchief to wear around your neck. We'll have a special ceremony in the courtyard to swear allegiance to Comrade Stalin and the Communist Party. Our great leader loves outdoor activities and wants you all to get lots of fresh air. We'll be playing games outside as often as we can."

The entire class cheers, and Max begins to play imaginary drums.

Then, without warning, Comrade Martha raises both her arms, and her basket slides down to her shoulder. She looks so funny with the basket dangling there next to her ear, and her arms up in the air as if she's Moses parting the Red Sea. But no one dares laugh.

"Long live the great Stalin!" she shouts. And we all repeat after her, "Long live the great Stalin!"

After Martha leaves, Comrade Minsky asks us to say our names one by one. But we can tell that he isn't really listening.

To my amazement, a tear rolls down his cheek.

I've never seen a teacher cry! I've never even seen a grown-up man cry.

Lucy raises her hand. "Are you homesick?"

Comrade Minsky is so startled by her question, he staggers backwards a little. She obviously got it right.

"Don't worry," Lucy says. "Everyone is homesick at first. When my grandmother came to live with us, she was homesick for ages. Then one day she looked out of the window and said, 'I'm not homesick anymore. You are where you are.'"

6

❦

Minus Numbers

Here is something interesting. You can have a number, like 2, but you can also have a number that is minus 2. Comrade Minsky taught us that.

What does minus 2 mean? I think it's more an idea than a number.

And you can actually subtract and add negative numbers!

minus 2 + minus 3 = minus 5

It makes sense. If I lose two marbles to Max, and then I lose another three, I've lost five altogether. Minus is something you had but lost. It only exists in the past.

I never knew arithmetic had a past and a present.

Losing marbles is what I'm doing at the moment. Max and I are shooting marbles in his front garden and he's mostly winning.

We're both in a good mood. We like our new school and we like our new teacher.

Comrade Minsky felt much better once he was

teaching us arithmetic. He said, "What clever children you are!" He seemed very happy about that.

Of course, not everyone in the class is clever. But he doesn't know that yet.

Suddenly, in the middle of our game, I sense that we're not alone. I've been so absorbed in trying to hold on to my best marble — the one that looks like spiraling stardust — that I didn't notice anything out of the ordinary, and neither did Max.

We both look up at the same moment and see my mother.

What's she doing here? I get the feeling she's been watching us for a while. Normally she interrupts our games without a second thought.

Now that I've spotted her, she smiles and says, "Darling, I just spoke to Max's mother and asked her if you could sleep here tonight. I'm afraid we have to move. Our poor old house is being borrowed for a while. Not forever. Just for now. The Russians need it for their bank."

Are my ears playing tricks on me? How can our house not be our house anymore? How can it be a bank? It doesn't look anything like a bank. It's a house!

My mother sits down on the crate that was our ship to Canada last week. She looks tired and her eyes are red.

"It's not just us. They've taken over lots of houses."

"But where will we live?"

"They're letting us stay in Mr. Jacobson's apartment, so we'll still have the same garden. Isn't that wonderful? Mr. Jacobson recently left town so it has all worked out."

Bruno the Bald is gone? Without even saying goodbye? He's lived in the side apartment of our house since before I was born. The low, arched door to his place always made me think of tales of magicians in the Black Forest. When Mr. Jacobson was away at work and Lana was washing his floors, I'd peek inside, half-expecting to discover a book of spells.

"We were very lucky," Mama continues. "We were given two hours to pack, and I managed to rescue all your things, darling. I've put them away for safekeeping. I took all our clothes, too, and the silver candlesticks."

I'm standing next to her and she reaches out and draws her arm around my waist. Right in front of Max! I pull away immediately. Luckily, Max's mother also embarrasses him with hugs and kisses when I'm around. Still. You have to draw the line somewhere.

"Safekeeping where?" I ask, hoping I haven't hurt her feelings.

My mother seems barely to have noticed. "Don't worry, Aunt Dora is looking after everything," she says, staring out at the fields. Her eyes glaze over as if she's forgotten where she is.

She comes out of her trance with a start and bounces up from the crate.

"I did manage to keep Clop-Clop for you," she announces proudly.

My heart sinks. Clop-Clop, my little wooden horse? That's the only thing that's not in storage?

Apart from my games and puzzles, I had three shelves of nature treasures: rocks, snakeskins, seashells, feathers, bird eggshells, a honeycomb, a piece of driftwood that looked like Albert Einstein ...

And what about my books? *Emil and the Detectives*, my Karl May collection, *Ancient Myths and Legends* — are they all gone?

I'm afraid to ask.

My mother reaches out to hug me again but stops herself and ruffles my hair instead. She was paying attention after all. Poor Mama!

"And, oh, Natt, guess what else? I almost forgot. They let us keep your bike. They've been taking bikes left and right for the army, but they let us keep yours. I expect it's too small for them."

So I'm supposed to be in raptures because I'm allowed to keep my own bike! Is this what war means? That you have to be grateful for smaller and smaller things? Any minute now I'll be expected to jump for joy because I don't have to sleep on a haystack.

Before Mama leaves, she hands Max a paper bag.

"That's for your mother," she says. Then she unlatches the gate, waves goodbye and hurries off. I feel a bit guilty, because I'm relieved that she's gone.

"What did one tricycle say to the other tricycle?" Max asks, to cheer me up.

But I'm not in the mood.

I don't have to look in the bag my mother gave Max to know what's inside. I can tell by the sweet almond smell that it's mandel bread. I'm not sure why it's called bread when it's actually a cookie. Maybe because each cookie is shaped like a tiny slice of bread.

I'm doing my best not to dig in right away, but Max beats me to it.

"Sorry about your house," Max says between mouthfuls. "Everything's gone topsy-turvy. One thing on top of another. My brother says the surreal is becoming real."

I look down at the marbles. They're lying motionless on the ground, waiting for us to shoot them out of the ring. The marbles are exactly where they were before my mother interrupted our game. Nothing has changed for them. War doesn't affect marbles.

I say, "If the house is minus one, and Bruno the Bald is minus one, together that makes minus two."

"But think of it this way," Max replies. "No more Iron Guard. That's plus a million. And no more Mrs. Bubu. That's plus a *billion*."

I can't help smiling. "Even though she was such a teeny-tiny peewee of a pipsqueak," I add, and we both roar with laughter. Mrs. Bubu wasn't much taller than me, and we were always shaking our heads at how such a small person could spew out so much evil.

Sleepovers with Max are usually crowded, with four of us in the big bed (actually a single and a double bed pushed together), but Max's two older brothers, David and Michael, are away. Michael is a really good artist, and the bedroom walls are covered with drawings of places, people and, in amazing detail, spiders spinning their webs. He has a thing about spiders.

Before we fall asleep, Max says, "I wish you had one of your Montreal letters here."

He means letters from my relatives. Whenever one arrives, Max and I devour every word. We try to imagine the tall buildings and the motor cars tearing up and down the crowded streets. And a single store that takes up an entire block, where you can walk for hours looking at bicycles, radios, gramophones, towers of chocolates, hundreds of magazines, every type of boot and shoe, and a thousand different games.

"I remember some things by heart," I say. "One building is twenty-six stories and —"

"Natt, listen." Max sounds serious, which is unusual for him. Very unusual. "I wish we were in Montreal this minute. Not because of the stores or the chocolates. But because the war is going to reach us soon."

"It will be okay," I tell him. "Mama says war is like a dog barking at a flock of birds who are sitting quietly on a haystack. The birds fly away, but then when the war ends, they come back to where they were."

"But what will happen in between? Where are David and Michael? Why did they leave in such a hurry? Why is everyone trying to sell their valuable things?"

People are selling their things? Well, that's news to me.

And you'd think I'd be the first to know, because most of the buying and selling takes place in a big empty field right next to our house. Every Tuesday and Thursday farmers and merchants arrive with their produce and goods piled high on wagons. The merchants bring toys, books, clothes, furniture and even, sometimes, a new invention, like sunglasses for kids.

Before the Russians changed our schedule, we'd be restless on Tuesday and Thursday mornings. We wanted to leave Hebrew school early so we'd have more time at the market. We'd try every excuse — headache, toothache, stomach ache, blurry vision, dizziness and, Max's favorite, "cloudy brain" — until finally Mr. Elias gave up and let us out at 10:00 a.m. instead of 11:00. That gave us two hours to explore and maybe pick up a treat.

"I thought the market was canceled last week," I say.

Max punches his pillow. I can tell he's worried about his brothers. Are they hiding? And if so, why?

"The grown-ups told us that the market closed down," he says, lowering his voice. "But it wasn't true. They didn't want us to go, because everyone is frantically trying to sell what they own. They say the market is going to be outlawed any day now, and they desperately need money, since the Russians are taking everything. I heard my parents talking about it."

Is that why my mother specifically told me to stay with Max after school last Tuesday and Thursday?

"If the war comes here," I say, "we have to be heroes."

Max doesn't answer. I'm not sure he heard me.

I look out of the bedroom window. I can see the Big Dipper and the North Star. The stars are exactly where they were last night and where they'll be tomorrow. They seem to be telling me that everything will be fine, fine, fine — like the old woman who tells your fortune at the market. Max and I used to eavesdrop on her through the back flaps of her tent. She'd peer into a crystal ball and predict wonderful things. She's the one who told Lana she was going to marry a rich man in the United States and have an enormous wedding cake. A few times the old woman's predictions made us laugh so hard that we had to run off before we were caught — like the time she told the Goat Man he'd find a treasure if he took a bath and buried his old clothes.

"What *did* one tricycle say to the other tricycle?" I ask Max. But he's already asleep.

7

Stormy Weather

Bruno the Bald's apartment is cozy (no book of spells) but it only has two rooms: a living room with a kitchen in the corner, and a tiny bedroom with a high narrow bed. So high you need a footstool to climb into it.

Mama said she'll look for something better, but in the meantime she asked me where I want to sleep. It makes no difference to me, so I told her I was fine with the two-seater in the living room. Papa can either squeeze in with her or sleep on a straw mat on the floor.

I can sleep anywhere. I once dozed off on a sack of potatoes in the shed. My parents were calling out my name, searching up and down, going mad with worry, but I didn't hear a thing. I was snoring away, dreaming about potato pancakes.

Speaking of food, Mama says we're going to eat supper at Aunt Dora's tonight. I don't say anything, but I'm secretly glad. I've heard more than one person refer to Dora as a culinary genius, and I have to agree.

"Where's Lana?" I ask. I haven't seen her since we moved out of the house.

"She had to go home," my mother replies. "But she'll visit as often as she can."

I must be hungrier than usual, because my first thought is how much I'm going to miss Lana's Friday treat — a lima-bean and vegetable dish she calls *fasoli*. She's the only one who knows how to make it.

It occurs to me that Olek and Zoomie have also vanished. As a matter of fact, all the men who helped my father with his grain business are gone. I decide not to say anything about it.

"Before we leave for Dora's, I have something to tell you," Mama says. "I'm afraid Hebrew schools aren't allowed anymore."

"Not allowed? Why not?"

Our Hebrew classes are more like club meetings than lessons. We adore Mr. Elias. We like his pretty wife, Cecilia, too. Halfway through the morning, she enters the room with a tray of thick slices of buttered bread and mugs of warm cocoa. We each get one mug and two slices of bread.

Mostly we learn Hebrew, which no one spoke in their daily life for hundreds of years — not since ancient times. But now it's being revived. We subscribe to a kids' magazine in Hebrew, and when it arrives we go over it page by page. We even wrote to the magazine last year and they wrote back, promising to publish our letter when our turn came. The letters are next to the joke page.

Uzi: Why do you wear glasses while you sleep?
Buzi: So I can see my dreams more clearly.

A boy in Tel Aviv to his friend: Hey, let's go to the cinema.
His friend: I don't have time, I have to help my dad do my homework.

Apart from Hebrew, we learn about the idea of a homeland for the Jews. This homeland is going to be in Palestine. Or at least that's the plan. It's not clear if it's going to work out.

We don't learn religion, though sometimes we discuss Bible stories. For example, should you kill someone who is beating a slave and bury him in the sand? (Max says yes, I say no.)

"The churches are closing down, too," my mother says. "For once it's not just the Jews."

She forces herself to laugh. It's a bit spooky, that type of fake laugh, especially when it's your mother who's putting on an act.

"But," she continues, "there are going to be secret classes three evenings a week. It's up to you whether you want to go."

So Hebrew school is not completely over! I have to admit that the idea of a secret school is kind of exciting.

"What are other kids doing?" I ask.

"Most are going, though not Max. His parents have five children, and a lot to think about right now."

Hebrew school without Max! It won't be nearly as much fun. Still, if other kids are going, I want to go, too. I can keep a secret.

"I definitely want to go," I say, "but is it okay if I don't go to *every* class?"

My mother bursts out laughing. This time her laugh is genuine.

On the way to Dora's, my mother says, "You know, Natt, one very lucky thing is that the Russians like Aunt Dora and Uncle Isaac."

"Don't they like everyone?" I ask. "Don't they like us?"

My mother says, "Well, let's see ..." Which means she's thinking of an answer.

Finally, she says, "You could say that they trust Uncle Isaac more than other people. When he was at university, he published an essay that impressed the Russians."

"Did he write about Karl Marx?" In school the walls are covered with posters of Marx, Lenin and Engels, fathers of the Communist Revolution. My favorite is Karl Marx. I like his wild hair and huge beard. And I like the fearsome way he puts things. *Proletarians have nothing to lose but their chains! Workers of the world, unite!*

"Actually, Uncle Isaac's essay was about the peasants' revolt in England in the Middle Ages." My mother chuckles. "By some miracle, it ended up on a list of revolutionary writings. In times of change, you want to be in the good books of whoever is in power."

As soon as we reach Dora's house, I see Papa walking toward us.

I run over and he takes my hand. I've missed him. He's been coming home after I'm asleep and leaving before I'm awake. He has swollen glands and a bit of a fever, but he says he can't stay at home because there's too much to attend to. I'm worried about him.

Supper at Aunt Dora's is a little disappointing. She couldn't make any of her usual dishes, as there was a problem "acquiring the ingredients." Instead she's prepared stuffed peppers and a big pot of barley and carrot soup. That's it for the main course, apart from bread.

But dessert — vanilla pudding — is as mouth-watering as usual.

"How's school these days?" my aunt asks me.

"Much better than before," I tell her. "Comrade Minsky is reading *War and Peace* to the class."

My aunt and uncle are astonished. "In Russian?"

they both ask. People in our family often say the same thing at the same time. I'm used to it.

"Yes, though he's more like telling us the story. He's a Jew, I think. I caught him listening when Lucy was talking to me in Yiddish, and I could tell he understood."

"I met him at the pharmacy," Uncle Isaac says. "He struck me as a very nice man. He told me a movie projector is coming to town."

My cousins, Faigie and Ottilie, practically fall out of their chairs with excitement. I'm praying my mother won't tell them the story of the train. She looks at me, and I shake my head. To my relief, she understands.

After supper, I join Faigie and Ottilie in their room. They're a few years older than me, and all they ever want to do is dress up and pretend they're cabaret performers while I, the audience, sit on a chair and watch them. It's boring.

Today is no exception. Faigie and Ottilie open their costume chest and pull out Japanese fans, glittery shawls, decorated hats, grown-up shoes. They twirl their skirts and flap their fans. Then they sit on chairs that are facing the wrong way, Marlene Dietrich style, and sing one of their favorites, "Stormy Weather" in German. *Ohne dich, without you …*

Without me is right. Unfortunately, my cousins' singing is the kind that makes dogs howl. I mumble some excuse and slip away. Maybe Aunt Dora will offer me another bowl of pudding.

To my surprise, the door to the kitchen is pulled to — not all the way, but almost. There's a tiny gap, and through it I hear the grown-ups whispering. I can't hear much at first, because my cousins are screeching away, but when they take a break to change costumes, I pick up a few words.

Illegal ... Bucharest ... eggs ... no food anywhere ... sold the candlesticks ... the telescope ...

The telescope!

That must be my telescope they're talking about, the one Mama said was in safekeeping. They've gone and sold it!

Max was right. They're trying to sell everything.

Tears form in my eyes. They probably sold my kaleidoscope, too, and my globe of the world and everything else. Even my books.

I want to dash out into the yard and kick the tree and run away and never come back.

Then I remember what Papa said about being a hero in wartime just by getting through the day.

This is exactly what he was talking about. Everything that's happening to us is part of the war situation. I can kick and shout. Or I can be a hero and get through it.

After all, my parents would never sell my treasures

if there wasn't a good reason. When the war ends, I'll get every single thing back.

In the meantime, I'm trying so hard not to cry that I get the hiccups. That always happens to me when I'm trying to hold back tears. I get the hiccups instead.

Very loud hiccups.

Uncle Isaac opens the door and sees me standing there, hiccuping. I've managed not to blubber, but my brimming eyes give me away.

"What is it, Natty?" my mother asks, hurrying over.

I have to think fast. I don't want them to know I was eavesdropping. And I don't want them to feel even worse about selling my things.

"It's Faigie and Ottilie. They …" Luckily, my hiccups give me time to think. "They wouldn't let me sing with them."

The grown-ups smile with relief. And sure enough, I end up with another bowl of pudding. I feel guilty, because it seems there's now a shortage of food, but Aunt Dora insists, and it would be very rude to refuse.

8

Natt the Statue

I dream that I'm falling down … down … and then, *Boom!* I really have fallen. I'm tangled up in sheets on the floor.

I manage to free myself and sit up.

Where am I? The room seems familiar …

Yes, I'm in Aunt Dora's living room. I've been sleeping on her sofa, and I've rolled onto the rug. But how come I went to bed at home and woke up at my aunt's?

And where are my parents?

Ice-cold dread grips me.

I begin to howl. I can't help it.

Aunt Dora rushes into the room. She's wearing her nightgown, which scares me even more. I've never seen my aunt in her nightgown and I don't want to. Only my mother is allowed to be in a nightgown.

My mother, who is probably dead.

"Hush, hush, Natt," Aunt Dora says. She tries to touch my shoulder but I pull away.

"Everything's fine," she promises me. "Your mother

had some things to do so she brought you here, that's all."

"Take me ... take me," I manage to say. She knows what I mean. *Take me to my mother.* I begin throwing on my clothes in a mad rush.

"Okay, just give me ten minutes," Aunt Dora says. "Everything is fine, Natt. Do you want some tea?"

I shake my head. I'm trying to button my shirt, but my fingers refuse to obey. I give up and tuck my unbuttoned shirt into my trousers. Then I grab my jacket, unlock the front door and step outside. I've stopped sobbing, but I'm still trembling like a leaf in a rainstorm.

So much for Natius the Musketeer.

I'm so desperate I almost call to my aunt to hurry up, but just then the door opens. Aunt Dora leads the way — to our apartment! I could have run there myself, if she'd told me that's where my mother was.

The small apartment is filled with people. I don't look at any of them. I wriggle my way to the bedroom and there's my mother sitting on the high bed, holding a large handkerchief and crying. Her friends are gathered around, trying to comfort her.

Where is my father?

"Like robbers, like robbers," my mother moans. "They took him in the middle of the night like robbers ..."

The minute she sees me, my mother stops crying. She looks at Aunt Dora as if to say, *Why did you bring him here? Didn't I ask you to keep him?*

But when Aunt Dora shrugs, my mother understands.

"Come here, my angel," she says, because I'm standing in the doorway, frozen. I've turned into a statue of Natt.

Someone lifts the statue up, carries it over to my mother and seats it on the bed.

"Your father is fine," Mama says, trying to smile. "He's been arrested. With a bit of luck, it won't be for long. They only want to ask him some questions. And he's right here in the town jail. What luck! They didn't send him to another city."

My father, in jail? How can that be? He's the sort of person who thinks not saying *How are you?* when you pass someone on the street is the equivalent of hitting them over the head with an umbrella. He once spent a week looking for the owner of a purse he found on a park bench. He refused to leave the purse, which was full of money, with the police. He didn't trust them. And he refused to give up. Which was a lucky thing, because the owner turned out to be a widow with five children.

I think of the town jail, which is also the courthouse. It's a long building, with four or five pointy roofs and rows of tall windows. It doesn't look scary.

"What did Papa do?" I ask. I can barely speak, and the words come creaking out like a broken grinding wheel.

"Nothing, absolutely nothing!" Mama exclaims. "The Russians want to make sure he isn't against them. That's all it is, darling Natt. They've arrested everyone who endorsed bank loans — over fifteen men, just last night."

"Maybe he could write an essay like Uncle Isaac," I suggest.

In spite of everything, my mother laughs. And then she kisses me right in front of everyone.

"My sweet little boy, you always cheer me up," she says. "And now, until Papa comes back, you're the man of the house."

If I'm the man of the house, why is she kissing me in public and calling me her little boy, for goodness' sake?

"How did you get me to Aunt Dora's?" I ask.

"Uncle Isaac came and carried you. You really are a deep sleeper," she says fondly.

Uncle Isaac places his hand on my mother's shoulder.

"Don't worry, Sophia," he says. "I'm going to put together a petition. We can easily get a hundred signatures. Everyone adores Shiku. I'll go to every town in the area. He's bailed out countless people. They can all share their stories."

My mother nods. "Thank you, thank you." She turns to address all her friends. "Thank you, everyone, for your kindness. I know you all have a lot to do. I'll be fine."

The apartment slowly empties. Only Aunt Dora stays behind. She helps my mother with breakfast, and we all sit down to eat semolina porridge and bread with jam. The bread is stale and the semolina is lumpy, but it's the last thing I care about. I'm just glad my parents are alive.

9

A Prize from Stalin

As I pack my schoolbooks, I begin to worry.

Not about Papa, because I'm sure he'll be released as soon as the Russians realize they've made a mistake.

But what will the other kids think? They've probably heard by now that my father's been arrested. In a small town like ours, it's hard to keep anything secret. Especially when it involves the police.

The truth is, I don't want people to think that I'm the son of a criminal.

I feel terrible about being so disloyal. And about thinking of myself instead of Papa.

Worrying slows me down, and I'm a few minutes late for class. I take my usual seat next to Max.

He leans over and whispers, "Are you okay?"

I nod. At least I can count on Max. He'll always be on my side, no matter what. Maximus and Natius — indivisible!

Lucy also reaches over. She drops a tiny homemade card on my desk: a drawing of a heart surrounded by rainbows and blue butterflies.

A heart! What does it mean?

I answer my own question. *It means she likes you, you ninny.*

Or maybe she's just being nice because of Papa. Either way, it feels as if the blue butterflies have flown straight from the card to my stomach. It's a good feeling, though, like dipping my toes in the river on a hot day.

It's going to be hard to concentrate on arithmetic. We're still on negative numbers. Apart from adding negative numbers, you can subtract, multiply and divide them.

Max raises his hand with a question, but before Comrade Minsky can answer, the door flies open and Comrade Martha bursts into our classroom. She's always breathless and red-cheeked when she enters a room, as if a strong wind has blown her in.

"Hello, children," she says. "*Dobroye utro.*" She's holding two thin packages wrapped in brown paper.

"*Dobroye utro*, Comrade Martha," we reply in a sing-song. For some reason, it takes much longer to say things in a group.

Comrade Martha can barely contain her excitement. "Our great leader Comrade Stalin has sent me two special prizes to give out today," she announces.

"It's for the boy and girl who have shown outstanding revolutionary spirit during the first weeks of school. The girl is … Mariana!"

Everyone applauds, and little Mariana, who cried when she heard we had to repeat grade four, looks startled and confused.

"Come up, Mariana, and get your prize."

Mariana, who now has shoes, walks up to the front of the classroom. She still looks confused and even a bit scared, but everyone cheers her on. Comrade Martha hands her a thin rectangular package, and she mumbles a thank you before hurrying back to her corner desk.

"And the boy who has shown outstanding revolutionary spirit is … Natt!"

Me? Did she say my name? I haven't done anything outstanding. But then, neither has Mariana.

There's more cheering as I rise to collect my prize. I don't have far to go, because my desk is in the front row.

Comrade Martha shakes my hand. I almost give a little bow as I thank her, but just in time I remember that Communists don't bow. We're all equal.

Max is beaming. He looks as if he's the one who won a prize, and not just any prize, but something huge, like a private soccer lesson with Giuseppe Meazza, or a lifetime supply of marzipan.

"Natt and Mariana are now one step closer to being Pioneers," Comrade Martha says enthusiastically.

"I'm very proud of them, and so is our great leader. Comrade Stalin is proud of you all. You are all going to bring honor to our revolutionary country."

What a relief! No one cares that my father is in jail. No one is going to hold it against me or talk about it. It's as if it never happened.

"And now we're going to learn a song," Comrade Martha says. She tries to teach us a Russian song, but she goes too fast and expects us to remember too much at once. We end up mumbling gibberish. The gibberish gets louder and louder. We're doing it on purpose now.

Comrade Martha turns a dark shade of red. "We'll have to practice some more," she says, looking confused and sounding, for the first time, a little at sea. I feel sorry for her. It's not her fault she's a bad teacher.

But a few seconds later she's in a good mood again, and before leaving the room she calls out, "*Za Rodinu, chest' i svobodu!*" At least those words we know. We learned them on our second day. *For the Motherland, honor and freedom.*

"Let's stay inside," Max says when it's time for lunch. "I'm tired. My body is tired and my brain is tired."

It's not like Max to be tired, but I'm more than happy to eat lunch in the classroom. I'm pretty exhausted, too, come to think of it.

We stay in our seats as the classroom empties. Comrade Minsky doesn't leave, either. He's not on playground duty today, so he has no reason to go out. I can tell he hates playground duty, probably because he's always cold.

I remove the string from my package and the brown paper flies open. Inside there's a very thin book. Max and I look at the book and start giggling. As we turn the pages our laughter gets louder and louder. Because it's a baby book! A baby book with about six pages and pictures on every page. Perfect for three-year-olds. Russian three-year-olds.

Comrade Minsky's curiosity gets the better of him. He walks over to my desk and picks up the book.

"Impossible!" he exclaims.

We weren't expecting this. Now it's our turn to be curious. What's impossible? That Comrade Martha thinks we'd be interested in a baby book?

But that's not it. As Comrade Minsky turns the pages, he mutters, "Daniil," in disbelief. "Daniil Kharms. How can that be? He was ..." He glances nervously at the door, then at the book, then at us, then at the door again. "He was a great ... a famous ... I mean he's written ..."

Every time he starts to speak, something stops him. It's almost as if he's afraid of Comrade Martha.

What can she do to him? He's too old to be a Pioneer.

He sits down at the empty desk next to us and, as if he's made up his mind about something, he says,

"Let me translate the charming poem in this book for you."

As he reads the poem, his voice begins to break. And before we know it, he's weeping.

"Please forgive your teacher," he says, taking a handkerchief out of his pocket and blowing his nose. "And please don't tell anyone I was upset. You're good little boys. I'm sure you understand. I have two children myself."

We both nod solemnly. We will never tell a soul that our teacher was crying over a book, not even our parents. A Musketeer's vow is set in stone. Don't ask me how we know that this is a Musketeer moment. We just do.

When the kids stream back into the classroom, everything appears to be the same. But it isn't. All this time, Maximus and I were pretend Musketeers. Now our task is real.

10

Natt the Nomad

For the past few weeks my mother's been too busy to look after me. She's like the prince in Cinderella, going from house to house and town to town. Not to find the owner of a glass slipper, but to collect signatures for the petition to free Papa.

In addition, she has to wait outside the jail every day, in a very long line, so she can give the guards a package of food or clothes for Papa. The guards work for the NKVD, the Russian secret police. Or maybe they *are* the secret police. All I know for sure is that the NKVD are the ones who arrested Papa in the middle of the night, and that everyone is scared of those four letters.

"The guards keep most of the packages for themselves," I heard Mama tell Aunt Dora. "All I can hope is that the cheese pies will dispose them to give Shiku special privileges."

In other words, a bribe!

As a result of all this, I've become a bit of a nomad. I have several camping sites:

Aunt Dora and Uncle Isaac: Sofa too narrow (afraid of falling off again), food good (though more repetitive than it used to be), cabaret songs ongoing (I am showing fortitude).

Aunt Frieda (a widow): Brand-new house, electricity, modern flush toilet, modern bath, not much to eat. The Russians took over her leather goods store and now pay her to run it, but she says the pay is barely enough to live on. Eight-year-old Cousin Leo has a whistling train set, which keeps us occupied for hours. It's the only train set in Zastavna.

Uncle Aaron and his wife Irma: Tiny apartment, Irma beautiful, cream cakes, have to sleep on floor rug.

Max: Perfect, but I feel bad eating their food and Max's mother won't take food gifts from my mother because of the situation with Papa.

My grandparents in Viznitsa: My grandparents treat me like a prince. We have picnics by the lake, followed by a game called badminton — a bit like tennis but easier. Unfortunately, the only way to get to Viznitsa is to take a train from Czernowitz. My mother has managed to arrange only one visit so far. I had to pretend to be the nephew of a couple with a travel permit.

But yesterday, when my mother picked me up from Aunt Frieda's, she informed me that she's found a permanent (for now!) home for me that "will solve all our food problems."

At first I was so hurt I felt a prickling behind my eyes. It sounded as if Mama was telling me that she can't find enough food for a boy who sometimes accepts second helpings, and who is a bit on the chubby side. And with Frieda and Leo right there in the room listening!

"I don't need second helpings," I told her. My voice was so low she had to ask me three times to repeat what I'd said. *"I don't need second helpings!"* I shouted.

"Oh, Natt!" my mother cried out, taking hold of both my hands. "I want you to have all the helpings your heart desires. You and Leo and Frieda and me … there isn't enough food for anyone these days. It's all going to the soldiers. And with so many men fighting, there aren't enough workers for the farms. In Czernowitz people line up for hours for a single loaf of bread. We're lucky here."

"I'm going to invent a machine that turns turnips into cake," Leo said, and the conversation moved, thankfully, to all the things we'd transform with Leo's machine.

I never thought of food running out before. I always thought food was like air — a part of life that was simply there. Maybe you could afford more, maybe you could afford less, maybe some things, like cashew nuts (which I've only had once, a memorable experience), are hard to come by. But the idea that food could vanish altogether never occurred to me.

It scares me, and for once I'm not embarrassed about being afraid. Anyone would be.

"The Shapiras are looking forward to having you," my mother continued. "With three young girls, they could use another man in the house. They're hoping you'll think of them as your honorary aunt and uncle."

I've been to the Shapira farm a few times, and I'm pretty excited about living with them. They built the house themselves, with rough loam bricks white-washed with lime, and a thatched roof, and a floor made of hard clay. It makes me think of olden days, when Sir Galahad, the greatest knight of King Arthur's Round Table, roamed the land in search of the Holy Grail. And I love the smell when you're inside — like wood or grass after it rains.

Mama says the Shapiras want to help us in any way they can because my father arranged for them to buy a milk processing house. That's what they call the brick building in the yard where various machines and gadgets separate milk from cream, press cheese and churn butter.

The milk comes from two large cows. Mr. and Mrs. Shapira also grow vegetables, which they store in a cellar deep under the ground. There are other things in the cellar, too, like jam and pickles and all kinds of preserved food. Mrs. Shapira makes cookies with the skin you get when you boil milk. It sounds crazy, I know, but they're delicious. And I'll be able to eat as many sunflower and pumpkin seeds as I want. They have whole sacks of them.

As for their three girls, who are aged one to six, they're cute and fun to play with, even if it's only baby games.

My life as a nomad is over. For now.

11

Switzerland

Max is in a bad mood.

It's Sunday afternoon and I've asked him to bring out the bag of marbles, but he doesn't want to play marbles or anything else. He's sitting on the crate in his front garden, scratching himself. He scratches his legs, his arms, his scalp.

"The bugs are driving me insane," he says. "I'm sure I have lice. And bedbug bites. And flea bites and mosquito bites and every other type of bite."

"Did your mother check you for fleas?" I ask.

"Yeah," he says with a half-smile. "Couldn't find any. She says it's all in my mind."

At least he's smiling again, even if it's not his usual all-out grin.

"I get that, too," I say. "I just hear the word *fleas* and I can feel them crawling through my hair." I begin scratching my scalp because, sure enough, my entire head is suddenly itchy.

Soon we're scratching ourselves and hopping

around the garden as if we've both gone loopy. We stomp and roll our eyes and throw our heads back and shake our arms and yodel and sing gibberish like we did in class when Comrade Martha tried to teach us that song.

Then we start spinning. We spin and whoop and go round and round until the entire world is spinning with us and we both fall to the ground because we're too dizzy to stay on our feet and we're laughing and out of breath and waiting for the world to stand still.

Max's twin sisters, Raya and Rita, come outside to see what's going on. Their aprons are sprinkled with flour and soot. They're only three years older than us, but they're in charge of all the cooking and baking.

"What's all this racket?" Raya asks.

The way you can tell the sisters apart is by their hair. Rita has long auburn braids that she winds around her head like a crown. Raya used to have long braids, too, and the two of them loved to fool everyone by switching identities. But last year Raya decided to cut her hair short like a Hollywood movie star. Now we all know which twin is which.

"Come inside," Raya says, waving us in with her long freckled arm. "We'll have tea. I have something to tell you."

We wipe the dust off our clothes and follow her inside, still a bit wobbly from all that spinning. I feel calmer now. Going loopy clears your head.

We sit at the kitchen table. It's just the four of us today. Max's mother has a job now, so she isn't home as much as before. And Michael and David are still away, though Michael sent Max a drawing of a man sleeping on a park bench with a newspaper over his face. The newspaper's headline says *Do Your Part*.

I notice that the silver teapot Max and his family were so proud of is gone. Raya pours the hot water into our mugs straight from the kettle.

Rita offers me sesame crackers, but I can tell they need the crackers for themselves.

"No, thanks," I say. "I'm still too dizzy."

"We have some good news," Raya tells us. She sits down at the table and twirls a strand of hair round her finger. She can't twirl it much, though, because her hair's so short now. I can tell it bothers her.

"We just received word," she continues, "that Father's been very, very lucky. A man he once helped has arranged for him and Michael to travel with him to Switzerland. I don't know the details, and you mustn't breathe a word to anyone. This man is someone important, and he's in poor health, so Father and Michael are going as his attendants. Once Father gets there, he's going to send us money so we can join him. So ... " She can't decide how to finish the story. "So we're on our own now."

Switzerland is the safest place in Europe at the

moment, because it's not in the war. The Swiss government decided to be neutral. They don't want to fight. Somehow, Hitler accepts that.

"What about David?" Max asks, as if he's daring his sisters to lie to him.

"David is safe. He might join the Russian army as a cook. They won't send him to the front because of his eyesight, but they need cooks. So you're the man of the house now, Max."

Exactly what Mama said to me! But Max thinks it's funny. He jumps up on his chair and pounds his chest like a gorilla. "I am the ruler of the universe, supreme chief and master of all beings, and whomsoever does not obey me shall have to answer to my sisters!"

Raya and Rita laugh, but I feel too sad to join in. I'm truly happy for Max's family, but Papa's arrest seems more unfair than ever.

That's the thing about war. When there isn't a war on, you make decisions, and if they're good decisions, you're fine, and if they're bad decisions, you pay the price. But in a war, even if you try to make good decisions, it's all a matter of luck. Max's father was lucky to have an important friend.

My eyes fill with tears as I think about Papa. No one is allowed to visit him, not even Mama. The jailhouse has lots of windows facing the street, but the cells are in the back of the building, so he can't see us, or anyone, even if we walk by.

Raya notices at once, and comes over to where I'm sitting so she can hug me. It's half-nice but also half-annoying (one mother is enough).

"Be brave, Natt," she says. "Do you want to stay over tonight? We have lots of room."

"I'm staying at the Shapira farm now, did Max tell you?"

"No, we didn't know. What's it like?' Rita asks.

"It's fun. They have a milk processing house. And I help out with their three little kids."

"Maybe Mr. Shapira can let you ride his cow," Max says. He does a very convincing *moooo* and this time I join in the laughter.

I think I've made up my mind about something.

It's clear that things are going to be bumpy for a while. Anything can happen these days.

But for me, it's going to be an adventure.

Not that I want bad things to happen. But seeing as there's a war, it's probably inevitable. That dog is going to bark at those birds.

Still, as long as I have Mama and Papa, I can put up with hardship. I'm done with being a scaredy-cat.

And I have my co-Musketeer, Maximus, by my side. *One for all and all for one!*

TWO

MINUS A TOWN

1941
SPRING

1

Dark Forces

It's my birthday in two weeks — April 1st.

Yes, I was born on April Fool's Day, and as a prank, the nurses told my mother that even though I was only a few hours old, I could already speak, and that I'd asked for milk while she was sleeping. She believed them!

I'm still living with the Shapiras, but at weekends I stay with Aunt Dora and Uncle Isaac. My mother is usually there when I arrive, and she hugs me as if I've been lost at sea for a year and everyone thought I was dead.

I've been putting up with it because I feel sorry for her. She stands in line every day at the prison, with packages for Papa, and she's still hoping to get him released.

Today, as soon as she's finished squeezing the breath out of me, she crouches down and whispers, "Guess what, Natty dear? My packages have finally paid off!"

Does she mean that her bribes have worked, and that my father is going to come home?

No, that can't be it. Even the petition to free my father didn't have any effect. Instead, Uncle Isaac, who submitted it, was accused of Coming to the Aid of an Enemy of the People and presenting a "forged document."

It wasn't forged! A hundred and seventeen people signed the petition.

Aunt Dora says it was a miracle Uncle Isaac wasn't arrested, and a miracle that the petition wasn't confiscated. All the people who signed it could have found themselves in deep water. The only reason the authorities let Uncle Isaac off the hook is that he's still in Stalin's good books on account of that essay he wrote long ago. Pure blind luck.

The worst part is that my father isn't an enemy of anyone. It's just a terrible mistake.

If only we could talk to him! But Mama isn't allowed to visit him in prison or even send him a note. And he can't look out at the street.

That's what my mother's news is about.

"Listen carefully," she says, lowering her voice. "One of the guards took pity on me — no doubt because they've all been eating so well, thanks to me. He took me aside and whispered in my ear that today Papa will be able to look out of the window. So, the two of us are going to walk by in exactly an hour!" Her face is flushed and her eyes are brimming with tears. Poor Mama.

"I will tell you where to look," she continues. "Papa misses us so much. And this may be his only chance to see us in a while. We mustn't stop, though. We have to continue walking slowly. No matter what, don't stop and don't wave. Just act as if we're there by accident. Otherwise the guard will get into trouble. Do you see what I mean?"

My mother, as usual, seems convinced that I'm four years old. *Yes, Mama, I get it. We're breaking the rules and we have to try not to get caught. Us, Papa, the guard.*

I keep my thoughts to myself and nod.

"What a kind guard!" My mother clasps her hands in gratitude. "You can see in his eyes what a kind man he is."

She expects me to be ecstatic. But the truth is, I'm not sure what I feel.

On the one hand, I want more than anything to see my father, even if it's only for a second and through a window on the other side of the street.

But on the other hand, I'm a Pioneer now.

Last week we lined up in the schoolyard for the Pioneer ceremony. I practiced the pledge until I could say it in my sleep.

I solemnly promise to passionately love and cherish my homeland; to dedicate my life to the people; to live as the Communist Party teaches me; to fight and never surrender; and to unfailingly carry out the glorious traditions of the Pioneers of the Soviet Union.

Comrade Martha thumped on a drum (she doesn't actually know how to play drums, but she did her best), and the flag was raised. When the adults, who were also wearing red Pioneer scarves, came over and fastened identical scarves around our necks with leather rings, I felt determined to live up to the Party's highest expectations.

I have become a part of a great cause — the end of exploitation of the poor by the rich — and I will devote my life to that cause.

Then we all sang the song Comrade Martha tried to teach us that day when she went too fast and we all sang gibberish. It's my favorite song now. It fills my heart with the beauty of our mission.

Dark forces oppress us
in the battle for which we are destined.
An unknown fate awaits us
but we will proudly, boldly raise
the banner of the workers' struggle …

I love Papa. I love him with all my heart. But as a Pioneer, how can I betray my oath of allegiance? It's strictly forbidden to Give Comfort to an Enemy of the People.

I'm sure Papa tried to explain that he's always believed in equality. He even belonged to a socialist group for a few years, but the group was devoted to the idea of a homeland for the Jews, so it doesn't count. The Russians are against the whole idea of Palestine.

Anyhow, that's why I'm not jumping for joy. I don't know what to say or think or feel.

I'm sitting at Dora's table, but I'm so distracted I wouldn't notice if an elephant walked into the room. My mother thinks it's because I'm taking in the good news, and she leaves me alone. Mama and Aunt Dora always have a lot to talk about anyhow. Their main subject is food: where to get it, how much it costs, how to make the most of it. Sometimes they mention Uncle Saul.

"Uncle Saul" is their code word for the underground market — buying and selling food secretly, without involving the Russian authorities. Even the soldiers buy and sell on the underground market. It's really dangerous, though, if you get caught.

At last we set out, walking at a slow pace so that we won't reach the prison too soon.

"Be casual," Mama reminds me in a whisper.

I know! I want to snap back. *You're the one checking your watch every few seconds!*

We reach the jail exactly on time and begin strolling down the opposite side of the street.

My mother squeezes my hand and says in a low voice, "Now, look at the top row of windows, the fourth window from the corner. There he is, do you see him?" She's breathless with excitement, and in spite of all her warnings, her eyes remain glued to the window. She can't help herself. Still, it's not unusual to investigate the jail as you pass by, wondering who's inside.

As for me — what I do takes me entirely by surprise. I don't plan it. It just happens.

I turn my head away from the window. Away from my father.

I feel my cheeks burning with shame. Am I ashamed of my father or of myself? I'm not sure.

The only thing I'm sure of is that I've never been so mixed up and miserable in my entire life.

Before I know it, we're on the next street. I had my chance and it's over. Too late now to change my mind.

I'm hoping Papa didn't notice. I'm hoping he thought I was just trying not to be conspicuous. But he must have seen me turning my head the other way. As if he's not sad enough, I've made him even sadder. What is wrong with me?

And we'll never get another chance. The guard isn't going to take that kind of risk twice, no matter how many cheese pies my mother gives him.

2

Nightmare

I can't sleep.

I'm lying on the narrow sofa in Aunt Dora's living room and all I can think about is Papa, and how I turned my head away from him.

I wish I could ask God to forgive me, but now I'm a Pioneer, and Pioneers don't believe in God. At school we have an Atheist's Booth, and everyone is expected to bring atheist poems and atheist quotes from famous philosophers.

Still, I'm desperate, so even though I don't believe in God, I recite a Friday-night blessing. *Baruch ata Adonai ...*

The Hebrew words take me back to when we were a family and lived together in our house and there wasn't a war.

Before long I'm crying my eyes out. I think about how everything has changed and what a horrible person I am.

The worst part is that Papa is the opposite of an

exploiter. His mother died of influenza when he was eight, and he went to stay with a widow who ran a women's hat shop. She was a distant family relative and had offered to take Papa in, but she turned out to be "a gargoyle come to life," as Papa put it. She gave him burnt food on purpose and called him Bumpkin Boy while ordering him around.

When he was thirteen, he'd had enough. He made his way to Czernowitz and began selling eggs. He had to pick them up from the farmers at 4:00 a.m. Little by little, year by year, he managed to improve his situation.

Until now. Now he has nothing. No visitors, no letters, not even a window to look out of. And how many of Mama's food packages reach him? Probably one a month, or less.

I think about how when I spilled hot cocoa on his account book, or when Olek left six loaves of bread out in the rain, Papa just sighed and said, "Never mind. We all make mistakes."

Papa is the nicest person on planet Earth. And I've betrayed him.

Somehow, eventually, I fall asleep on Aunt Dora's sofa, only to have the worst nightmare of my life.

The nightmare is about a juggler I once saw. Every summer the circus comes to town and tents go up in the marketplace. Mama always tries to stop me from going. She says I could end up catching a dreadful disease because of the huge crowds and because the circus travels from place to place, picking up all sorts of dangerous microbes along the way.

I nod. And then I go anyway.

But one time, even though everyone said the circus was coming, the only performer who showed up was a dusty old man dressed in a clown costume. He was juggling three rings (which even Max can do) and trying to coax his skinny dog to jump through a hoop. He was so pitiful that we dropped all the money our parents had given us for treats into his donation jar. It didn't look like anyone else would donate anything.

That's what my nightmare is about: the dusty juggler. Except that in my dream Papa is the juggler. I keep hoping no one will notice him and I direct people to another part of the market. But at the same time I'm worried that no one will give him any coins because I'm keeping everyone away.

Then the rings Papa is juggling turn into marbles, and the marbles spill and scatter all over the ground. Papa tries to collect them and I try to help him, but they slip through my fingers. And now that I'm closer I see that it isn't a dog Papa is trying to steer through the hoop. It's a giant rat!

I think I'm going to vomit. I begin to run, desperately looking for a place to throw up, but my running makes the NKVD take notice, first of me, and then of Papa, and they arrest him because the rat won't jump, and I want to shout, *Can't you see it's a rat, not a dog!* But my voice refuses to work, and no matter how hard I try to call after him and tell him that I love him and that I'll come to see him, I can't get my throat to make the sounds.

I wake up drenched in sweat and sick to my stomach. I spend most of the day on the sofa, pretending to have a headache. I'm not even hungry.

On Sunday I drag myself to school, weighed down by my heavy heart and all the books in my bag. The Communist Party gave us identical leather schoolbags with a strap that goes across our shoulders, and we each have to work one hour a month, either cleaning or helping a teacher, to pay the Party back.

In the schoolyard, the main topic of conversation is a movie that's supposed to be coming to town.

Yes, we now have a cinema. Well, really just a room in the synagogue, which has been transformed into a Community House. The Russians brought a movie projector to town to teach us about the struggle of the proletariat and all the good things Communism is doing: building factories and dams, teaching peasants to read and write, bringing electricity to the masses.

But tonight we'll be getting a real movie. Everyone is trying to guess what it's going to be. Charlie Chaplin? The latest Greta Garbo? The kids who have been to Czernowitz in the past few weeks are being grilled on the films playing there.

I'm the only one who isn't excited. I don't deserve a movie. I don't deserve anything.

At snack time Max and I go to our usual corner in the Lenin Room. That's what our assembly hall is now called. At one point, Comrade Martha had this crazy idea that we'd all share our snacks. I could have told her it wouldn't work out. Kids don't like food from other kids' homes. The boys complained, the girls cried, the six Kaplan kids thought they'd be struck dead if they even touched the ham, and our best goalie, Martin, actually threw up after taking a bite of jellied cow's tongue.

So Comrade Martha had to abandon her idea.

I decide to tell Max about turning my head away from my father. I have to tell someone or I'll lose my mind.

"What sort of person would do something that awful," I moan.

"I'm sure he thought you were showing off your new haircut," Max says, grinning.

"It isn't funny!" I shout, and immediately feel myself flushing. I hate arguments, and whenever I contradict someone I get hot. According to Max, who finds it amusing, my face turns as red as a beet.

Max goes on grinning — I don't think he can help it — but he says, "I'm sure he assumed you were playing it safe. He assumed you did it so you and your mother wouldn't be conspicuous, seeing as you were supposed to be *by total coincidence* just promenading down that street at the exact moment he was at the window."

"Oh, why, why, *why* didn't I look at him?"

"Easy, *Mein Herr*. Because you miss him too much." Max puts on a frown and strokes an imaginary beard. "As you are no doubt aware, I have studied with the great Doctor Sigmund Freud."

When Max does one of his imitations, it's impossible not to smile.

And maybe it's true. Maybe seeing Papa would only make not seeing him worse, and that's the real reason I didn't look at him.

Maybe I'm even mad at him, in a way. I mean, it's not his fault he got arrested. But the thing is, three days before he was arrested, he wondered whether we should move temporarily to Bucharest. To my secret relief, he decided against it.

"If only we'd gone to Bucharest for a month or two," I say, shaking my head. "Papa would never have been arrested."

Max, who's been chomping on a carrot, freezes mid-chew, and his eyes widen behind his glasses.

What have I said?

Finally, he swallows. "I didn't know your parents were considering Bucharest," he says, and starts scratching his chest and arms more furiously than ever.

"What is it?" I ask. "Are you okay?"

"I'm glad you stayed here," he says at last. He leans back in his chair. He looks so small suddenly, like a little elf peering out from behind a leaf. "The Iron Guard has been going crazy in Bucharest. There wasn't a thing about it in the Russian newspapers, but word got around. Open your eyes, Natt. Open your ears and your eyes. You won't be safe unless you know what's happening around you. You can't live in a dream world forever."

That's the second time today Max has hurt my feelings.

And what he's saying doesn't even make sense. Listening to the BBC is no longer allowed, and the Russian-controlled newspapers don't mention the war or anything else. That means the adults have no way of knowing what's going on.

And if the adults don't know, how is a kid supposed to know?

3

Poor Wayfaring Stranger

I'm twelve today, and when Comrade Martha calls me away from class, at first I think it has something to do with my birthday.

But that can't be it. Other kids have had birthdays, and they weren't called out.

I'm not very happy about leaving, because we're right in the middle of *War and Peace*. Every day Comrade Minsky reads us another chapter. I don't want to miss any of it, but I have no choice. Comrade Martha is standing in the doorway with her usual cheery smile, waiting for me to join her.

Comrade Minsky grasps the problem at once.

"Natt," he says, "we're going to review our spelling until you return."

His words instantly lift my spirits. It's not just that I won't miss what happens when Napoleon comes across Andrei lying wounded on the ground after battle. It's that my teacher is ready to change the schedule just for me.

I've never been summoned by Comrade Martha before, and as I follow her I start to feel nervous.

What if something's happened to my mother?

I follow her to her office, which is really just a corner of the Lenin Room, sectioned off by two boards covered with Communist Party posters. There are posters all over town, along with banners, slogans and loudspeakers that repeat the same messages as the posters. The words collide in my mind like meteors in outer space — *Power to the Soviets, Follow the True Path, Long Live the Socialist Revolution, Communist Youth to Tractors, With Guns We Will Defeat the Enemy, With Hard Work We Will Have Bread …*

I suddenly feel so sleepy. Comrade Martha sits behind her desk, and I sit on the chair facing her. I hope I can keep my eyes open.

She folds her hands together and says, "First, Natt, I want to commend you on the wonderful work you've been doing. We're very, very proud of you. You could be working a little more on your sports, but your participation in our chess club, your academic grades, your revolutionary attitude and your top scores in Russian make up for that. If you keep it up, in four years you will be accepted into the Young Communist League. That is a very high honor. The next step is the highest honor of all: membership in the Communist Party."

"Thank you," I say politely, and do my best to stifle a yawn.

Why am I so tired suddenly? I could sleep for a week, or maybe a year. From up close I can see two black teeth at the back of Comrade Martha's mouth.

Like a witch — the words float through my jumbled thoughts.

"I just want you to keep in mind that no matter what happens, we are proud of you and of your accomplishments. You are a true asset to the Party."

No matter what happens? What does she mean?

But I'm afraid to ask, partly because if there is bad news, I don't want to hear it from her, but also because I'm too exhausted for any more news, good or bad.

I thank Comrade Martha and return to class, but I can't focus on *War and Peace*. I bury my head in my arms and doze.

Comrade Minsky wakes me by ringing the little brass bell he keeps on his desk. I'm the only pupil left in the classroom. Even Max, who either couldn't wake me or didn't want to, has gone home.

"Are you feeling well, Natt?" Comrade Minsky asks. "Anything I can help you with?"

"Thank you, but I just needed a nap," I say groggily, and I shuffle down the hall.

Even though it's a Tuesday, my mother is waiting for me across the street. On regular schooldays, I bike to Max's in the morning, park my bike at his place and walk with him to school. Then after school we walk back to his house, and just before suppertime I bike to the Shapiras'.

But tonight I'm supposed to have a birthday dinner at Aunt Dora's. I assume that's why my mother is picking me up.

When Mama sees me, she waves me over, takes hold of my hand and begins walking very quickly. She's wearing sunglasses, her hat is lowered over her forehead, and the collar of her coat is turned up all the way to her cheeks. She looks like a spy on the cover of a mystery novel.

I can tell she doesn't want me to say anything. Besides, she's walking too fast for conversation. We turn a corner and then another, until we reach a tall hawthorn hedge.

My mother pulls me behind the hedge, kneels down, wraps her arms around me and bursts into tears.

"Papa's had his trial in Czernowitz." She takes a hankie out of her pocket and blows her nose. "They all did. They were taken to the city last night and they all had their trial together. I just found out an hour ago, from Bertie's wife. There were witnesses and documents — everything was faked!" She's whispering, but she can barely control her indignation. "It was all invention! Oh, Natt, he's been sentenced to five years in … in …" She's too upset to continue.

"At least he's okay," I say. When your mother is

96

crying, you don't have time to think about how you feel. "And he's with his friends."

My mother stands up and blows her nose one last time. I feel an asthma attack coming on, but I force myself to breathe slowly. That's all my mother needs now — a kid with breathing problems.

"I'm sorry, Natt," she says. "I shouldn't be crying. Five years will fly by. He'll be safer in prison than in the army. Maybe he'll be let out early. And we have your birthday dinner tonight!"

"Can't we postpone it?" I ask. "I'm tired, Mama."

"But Dora's been cooking all day! Papa wouldn't want us to mope and be gloomy. Let's think happy thoughts."

At my aunt's place I curl up on the sofa and half-listen to the list of things Papa's been convicted of: being a counter-revolutionary, an Enemy of the People, an exploiter of the proletariat and a member of an illegal organization — the socialist group he once belonged to, where they discussed a homeland for Jews — even though it wasn't illegal when he belonged.

I slide into a dream. A clock wonders whether Papa will be allowed visitors now that he's had his trial.

"Bring him a minute hand to cheer him up," the clock says with a wink.

My mother's voice reaches me from a great distance. "Natt, wake up! Max and his sisters are here."

I rub my eyes and sit up.

"Happy birthday, Natius!" Max says, handing me a package wrapped in newspaper. "It's from all of us. Don't open it until after we leave."

Max knows I didn't really want a birthday party. Not without Papa. But my mother insisted.

And it's not much of a party, really. Just dinner with Max and his sisters. Their mother was invited, but she has a cold.

Rita and Raya kiss me. Rita recently exchanged her long auburn hair for four eggs, a cup of sugar and a bag of flour. Now she and her sister have identical haircuts again and I'm back to not being able to tell them apart.

Dora has prepared a feast, by war standards, with a small strawberry cheesecake for dessert.

When we've gobbled up every last crumb, Max taps his glass. He says, "Hear, hear!" and stands up on his chair.

"Ladies and gents!" he proclaims. "Welcome to Natt's Birthday Variety Show. I will open proceedings with a riddle.

"A bridge of pearls rises
Above a misty sea ..."

The adults interrupt with cries of "Schiller! 'The Rainbow'!" and they join in:

"Appearing in an instant —
It hovers dizzily.

"Water-logged it vanished
As when a stream goes dry.
Tell me how this bridge was built
And where its beauty lies?"

Everyone applauds as Max removes an imaginary hat and bows several times. Then he continues in his best master-of-ceremonies voice: "Right. Who will be next?"

My cousins, Faigie and Ottilie, jump up and shriek, "Us, us! We have something new! 'Wayfaring Stranger' in five languages, including English. Hold on, we just have to get our costumes."

Dora makes another pot of tea and we move back to the living room to wait for the two stars.

My cousins, dressed in their usual shawls and trinkets, make their entrance. They start off in English, as promised.

"I'm just a poor wayfaring stranger
Traveling through this world of woe."

Ottilie raises her arms to the heavens, and Faigie falls to her knees. At the same time, they're hopelessly off-key, and they sound like runners-up in a lamb-bleating, geese-honking, rooster-crowing competition.

We can't help it. We start laughing. Our laughter gets wilder and wilder. Before long, it's turned to weeping. We hug each other and no one's embarrassed and no one is trying to stop. We're sobbing our hearts out. Even Max.

The only ones who aren't crying are Ottilie and Faigie. They look quietly satisfied that their performance has had the desired effect.

4

Gulag

Max's gift is his father's large leather-bound doctor's diary. Only the first three pages are filled in. I can use the rest of the notebook to record daily events.

At the top of each page Max has added a joke. I finally find out what one tricycle said to another tricycle. *(I can't wait till I'm two.)*

But I won't be able to thank him for the gift today, because he's absent. When I arrived at his place in the morning, before I had a chance to climb off my bike, Rita came out and asked me to tell the school that Max has "congestion and a high fever." I'm guessing he caught his mother's cold.

School isn't the same without Max. But as soon as I take my seat, Lucy's sweet, soapy scent improves my mood. She leans over and whispers, "I heard about your father being sent to Siberia."

Siberia?

"Oh, no," I correct her. "He's coming back to our

jail." Which is what I assumed because ... because, why not?

She looks confused. "That's not what my father told me, but he must have got it wrong."

Comrade Minsky enters the classroom and our lesson starts, but my mind keeps wandering back to Papa. Now that I think of it, no one actually said anything about Papa coming back here. But ... Siberia? Siberia is a vast, uninhabited area, thousands of kilometers away. It's mostly ice and snow, and so cold the ground never thaws, even in summer.

Only serious criminals, like murderers, get exiled to Siberia.

I send Lucy a note:

Tell me everything your father said.

Comrade Minsky sees me passing the note to Lucy, but he doesn't mind.

She writes back.

He said your father is being sent to work in the gold mines in a place called Magadan. We can look it up.

I nod, and after school, in Lucy's living room, that's what we do. We look up Magadan in the atlas and find out it's more than 11,000 kilometers away! That's like crossing the Atlantic Ocean three times. And it's very, very cold there.

I can't imagine my father working in a gold mine. Maybe he'll be in charge of accounts.

"My dad says the Siberian prisons are called gulags now," Lucy says, gazing at me with big sympathetic eyes.

Gulag.

My father is going to a gulag. A word I didn't know until today is suddenly the most important word in my life.

"What exactly is that? Did he say?"

"A new type of prison. The NKVD run it."

"My father didn't do anything bad," I fume. "He's innocent!"

Lucy takes my hand and my heart leaps in spite of everything.

"We're all on your side," she says. "Would you like a slice of honey cake?"

I'm too impatient to wait until Max gets better to talk to him about what Lucy told me. I don't care if I catch his cold. So even though he's absent again on Thursday, I make my way to his house after school.

I find him sorting wood for the stove, separating the logs according to size. Both of us have to do chores now — Max at home, and me at the Shapiras'. Those were the good old days, when we barely had to lift a finger.

"You look good for someone with a high fever," I say.

Max shakes his head. "I don't have anything. I just didn't feel like going to school. And my sisters and mother need me at home. But don't tell anyone. Not even Lucy."

He drops a heavy log on the big-log pile. It rolls to the floor with a thud.

"Lucy says my father is going to a gulag in Siberia."

Max nods. "I thought you knew."

"The entire trial was a farce!" I exclaim.

"Well, don't say that to anyone," Max advises. "Or you'll be sent to the Gulag, too."

"No, Stalin likes children."

"Only obedient ones." Max snaps a twig in two. "But don't quote me on that. In fact, whatever you do, Natt, don't criticize anyone or anything. Promise me. You're too trusting."

"But we're supposed to be honest." I can feel my face going red again.

"No no no no no!" Max pretends to pull out his hair. "Honesty is NOT the best policy. Not now. Maybe some day. Maybe after the war. But for now, lie through your teeth. Lie, lie, lie! Tell them what they want to hear. Everything is good! Stalin is the greatest man the world has ever known! Got it?"

I nod. It's out of character for Max to lecture anyone. But I can see how frightened he is. Yes, for once Max is the one who is scared.

"I'm going to make you a list of who you can trust," he says. He finds a scrap of paper in a drawer and scribbles on it. "Memorize this," he orders.

I read what he wrote:

Your parents
My parents, sisters, brothers and me
Dora and Isaac (not their kids — too flighty)
Mr. and Mrs. Shapira (not their kids — too young)
Comrade Minsky (but never at school)

"Never at school? Why not?" I ask.

"Because there's always someone around the corner, someone you haven't seen. Even in the playground. That goes for everyone, everywhere. You have to be completely sure that no one can hear you."

"What about all my other relatives?" I ask.

"Stick to the list, comrade. Makes life easier. For goodness' sake, Natt. How many people do you need to whine to?"

I'm too insulted to answer. I'm not a whiner.

"You have to promise. I mean it." He clutches my shoulder and shakes me.

"Okay, okay, I promise. Only people on the list. My shoulder would be grateful if you stopped shaking it."

"Sorry, Natt. And I'm also truly sorry about your father," he says, rubbing his eyes behind his little round glasses. "But he'll be okay. The Gulag isn't so bad."

He looks down at the pile of wood and nervously pushes his glasses back to the top of his nose.

I have a sneaking suspicion that my friend Max is taking his own advice and, for some reason, not being totally honest with me.

5

Mr. Elias

It's the first of May. We just had our May Day cele-
brations — an entire day devoted to singing, dancing
and games, in honor of International Workers' Soli-
darity. Too bad Max missed all the fun. He stayed at
home with another one of his made-up illnesses. This
time it was a "dislocated collarbone." I think he finds
these ailments in his father's old notebooks.

It's sunny and warm out. A perfect day for bik-
ing, but I no longer have a bicycle. My knees kept
banging into the handlebars and I finally had to face
the fact that my bike was too small for me. I've had
what they call a growth spurt. I'm changing in other
ways, too, I've noticed. Good ways, which Max has
explained in fascinating detail.

Anyhow, my old bike is perfect for Cora, the eldest
Shapira girl, so I gave it to her. For now I'm on foot.
It's nearly dinnertime, and I'm headed home. The
Shapira house really does feel like home at this point.

I pretend that my parents live there, too, but are away on business.

Mr. and Mrs. Shapira say I'm the son they've always wanted. I've even learned how to look after a baby. She's funny, that baby, wobbling on her little fat legs, pointing to things she wants, smiling all the time. Her name is Mitzi.

Anyhow, walking turns out to be a lucky thing, because on the way I run into Mr. Elias, my old Hebrew teacher. I haven't seen him in ages.

I'm still mad at Mrs. Pumpernickel, his sister-in-law. She's the reason I left the secret Hebrew school.

Mrs. Pumpernickel isn't her real name. It's what we call her behind her back, because pumpernickel is our least favorite bread (hard, grainy, bitter) and she's our least favorite person (mean). She lives with Elias and his wife, and Mama says she's a dressmaker, but whenever we see her she's sweeping. She whisks the broom around as if she wants to sweep away not only the dust, but everyone who's in her way.

On the day I became a Pioneer, I ran straight from the ceremony to Aunt Dora's. It was a Friday, and I wanted to show my mother my red kerchief.

But no one was home at Dora's. Ever since the Russians took over, the grown-ups have been very busy, though I'm never clear on exactly what they're doing.

I remembered that a long time ago Mr. Elias lent Faigie and Ottilie a book of Hebrew songs by Bialik. It was still on their bookshelf.

I decided to return the book to Mr. Elias and share my Pioneer news with him at the same time. I hid the book inside my school bag, just in case. Hebrew isn't really allowed anymore. Only Yiddish is allowed.

I hurried over and knocked on the door. Mrs. Pumpernickel answered.

"Your teacher isn't here," she snapped. She grabbed her broom, which was leaning on the wall behind her, and began to sweep.

Before I could stop myself, I said, "You are talking to a Pioneer of the Soviet Union!"

She swung her arm and struck me, slapping my face so hard that I almost fell backwards.

No one had ever, ever slapped me before, and for a few seconds I literally had no idea what had just happened.

The pain wasn't nearly as bad as my shock. As soon as I regained my balance, I turned around and ran home, tears streaming down my cheeks.

I never returned to Hebrew class. It wasn't Mr. Elias's fault, but I just couldn't face that house again. I haven't seen him since.

Until now. He's leaving Mr. Mendl's candy shop with a small package. That store used to be packed with goodies — soda drinks with syrup, cookies, cake, ice-cream cones. But the shelves are mostly empty now. Even the ice cream is gone.

"Natt! Natt!" Mr. Elias calls out.

I'm embarrassed at first, because I left his class without any explanation or goodbye. But I can tell that he's happy to see me. I realize that he doesn't know about the slap. How would he? The only person I told was Max, and Max doesn't go to Hebrew school, either.

"I'm so glad to see you, Natan," Mr. Elias says.

Hearing my Hebrew name brings back a flood of memories. The kids' magazine, the jokes, the cocoa and buttered bread …

"I was just buying what passes for oat biscuits these days…. Listen, I heard about your father. I'm so sorry. You can't imagine. I love that man, simply love him. If only … still, what will be, will be. Better the Russians than those Nazi madmen."

He sighs and shakes his head. "The Russians are living in Cloud Cuckoo Land if they think Hitler will keep his word. He's making total fools of them. Any day now he's going to break the pact. Believe me, we're a thousand times safer with the Russians. But the Nazis are getting closer every day, heaven help us. Heaven help us."

I'm a little shocked, after Max's warnings, at how Mr. Elias is talking to me right there in the middle of the street. I'm also surprised that he's telling me, a kid, all these things that other adults seem to be trying to keep from me.

In fact, he looks a bit feverish. He's talking very fast and there's something wild about the way he's staring into the distance.

"Are you feeling all right, Mr. Elias?" I ask him.

"What? Oh, yes, I meant to write to Max and let you both know that the photos are ready. I finally made copies for everyone. The photo we took last year, remember? An artifact of history, now that Hebrew classes are a thing of the past …"

A thing of the past?

"You aren't giving classes anymore?" I ask. "I mean, I had to stop coming for other reasons, but no one told me they'd ended."

"That's right, no one is talking. Everyone is afraid. Their plan is working. *Don't talk, don't think. Obey.* We were found out, and that was the end of the class-es. By a miracle, no one was arrested." He breathes a sigh of relief, then grasps my arm. "Read Kafka, Natt. When you're a little older, read Franz Kafka. He saw it all. He saw it coming. Though even he could not have predicted this. Well, enough of that. As I said, what will be, will be. Come, we'll get you that photo."

Praying I won't run into his sister-in-law, I follow him to his house. Then, suddenly, I don't care if I run into her or not. She's just a skinny woman with a broom.

Still, I'm glad to find that she's away.

Mr. Elias offers me some borscht and we sit at the small kitchen table with our bowls. It's cold borscht, and very plain. No sour cream, no potatoes, no flavor other than the beets. Not even bread. *A sad borscht for a sad teacher* — the words pop into my head.

"Thank you, Mr. Elias," I say.

He sinks back in his chair. "No Mr. I'm just Elias now, God help me. If there *is* a God, which unfortunately seems not to be the case. I'd offer you an oat biscuit but I promised my daughter a treat. My wife will be sorry she missed you. She's taken Shainie to a puppet show. Stalinist hogwash, but Shainie won't know." He shuts his eyes. I have the feeling he hasn't slept in a long time.

But he's too wound up to rest for more than a few seconds. His eyes snap open and he jumps up from his chair and sprints out of the kitchen. He returns with the class photo and hands it to me.

There I am, the only boy with a tie. That's because I'm in my Scouts uniform, which I decided to wear for the occasion. Being a Scout is another part of my life that's gone. Scouts aren't allowed in the Soviet Union.

"Wait, wait." Elias runs to his study and comes back with a book called *The Trial*. It's by the writer he mentioned, Franz Kafka. The title makes me think of Papa. Part of me wants to read the book, but another part is scared of what I might find there. "You're too young now," Elias says. "But one day …"

He rummages around for a pen and inscribes the book. There's already an inscription on the title page, but he writes another one under it.

To Natt, with great affection and the hope that we will meet again when these dark clouds lift.

Then he pauses, thinks for a moment, and adds:

Kafka saw that the Nazis were headed our way. He did not know that the great Stalin would come to save us.

"That's to protect you," he says. "Stalin is a psychotic murderer, but let's not tell anyone."

Before I leave, Elias hugs me.

"Be safe, dear boy," he says. "Be safe. Somehow, we must try to make it through this war."

6

A Boy in Prison

We're sitting at the edge of our seats listening to Comrade Minsky tell us about the duel between Pierre and Dolokhov in *War and Peace*. The suspense is almost unbearable. I don't want Pierre to die! I really like Pierre, even if he's not perfect. And Dolokhov is wicked. It was his idea to tie a policeman to a bear — a real, live bear — and throw them in the river. And he was horrible to Pierre at the dinner party, where the fight began.

And then the strangest thing happens.

Suddenly, it's as if we're in the story. Right inside *War and Peace*. Because when we come out of school, the playground is filled with soldiers and army vehicles. The whole place has been transformed into a military campground. There are even tents and field kitchens.

How did they manage to set it up so fast without us noticing?

The minute Max sees the army camp, he grabs my arm and pulls me after him. The other kids stand

and watch the soldiers bustling among the trucks and tents, but Max is acting as if getting away is a matter of life and death, and he doesn't stop pulling me until we reach his house.

By then my chest is tight and I'm wheezing. I want to ask Max what's going on, but I need to catch my breath first.

No one else is home. Max pours me a glass of water from a tall jug, and when my breathing finally returns to normal, he says, "Listen. Some people from Poland called by here yesterday to warn us that the Soviet police have started arresting the families of Polish men who've been sent to the Gulag. They might do the same thing here. That means they could come after you, Natt — and your mother. You have to hide, or they might send you to Siberia, too. Wait here."

He dashes out, and I hear him banging around in the living room. When he reappears, he's holding what looks like a small furry animal. It turns out to be a fur hat with extremely long earflaps that tie under the chin.

He slides it on his head and we both burst out laughing.

Max shakes his head from side to side, and the flaps swing like horses' tails.

"My great-aunt made it when her rabbits died," he says. "No one in our family has the courage to wear it in public. But listen, it's the warmest hat on earth. Take it, and don't let it out of your sight. If you do end up in Siberia, you'll need it."

"Thanks, Max. But why would they send the families to Siberia? So we can be together?"

"Well, with any luck you won't be going anywhere," Max says. "But maybe you should stay at the Shapiras' for now. Skip school for a few days."

What is wrong with Max, who used to laugh at everything? My old musketeer friend Maximus has been replaced by a completely different boy. A boy who is jumpier than Zoomie these days.

Max drops five potatoes into a pot. "Always boil potatoes with the peel on, and then slide the peel off when they're cooked," he advises. "If you peel them raw, you lose too much of the potato."

He sits down at the table with a bowl of walnuts and begins cracking them open with a wooden nutcracker. I'd offer to lend a hand, but there's only one nutcracker in the house now. The silver one from pre-Russia days is gone.

"Why don't you read something out loud?" Max suggests. "I'll do the walnuts, and you'll provide entertainment."

On my way to look for a book I nearly bump into my mother, who must have let herself in through the back door.

"Oh, thank God I found you!" she exclaims.

"Listen, Natty." She looks imploringly into my eyes. "I'm going away for just a few days. You'll be fine with the Shapiras. If anyone asks you where I am, just tell them I went to visit friends. I'll be back soon, I promise."

"Okay." I'm not sure what the big deal is. I never see her during the week anyhow.

She kisses me a few hundred times and runs off without even saying hello to Max.

I read a few pages of *The Three Musketeers* to Max, and when his sisters come home, I take off. I don't mind the long walk to the Shapiras'. It's a warm spring day, and the fields are a sea of purple and yellow and blue wildflowers. You wouldn't think, looking at the fields and trees and sky, that there's a war. Nature doesn't get involved in wars. It's neutral, like Switzerland.

I get back in time to help bring in the cows, tidy up in the milking shed and play with Mitzi while Mrs. Shapira hangs laundry on the clothesline. I cover Mitzi with a towel, then take it off and say *peek-a-boo*. She laughs her head off every single time. How is it possible to find the same thing funny over and over?

I mash Mitzi's food and we play "here comes the airplane" — the food is the plane flying into her mouth. Then I shake out the rugs, feed the cats, get into pajamas and fall asleep the second my head hits the pillow.

❖

Loud noises never wake me up. I could sleep through an earthquake. Once I'm asleep, my brain is off-duty for the next eight hours.

But this is different. This sound is impossible to ignore.

Someone seems to be kicking the front door as well as pounding on it with their fists. A voice booms out, "Open up, open up!" in a very scary NKVD way.

Mr. Shapira dashes to the door in his pajamas and nightcap.

Four men carrying rifles and bayonets march into the room. One of them points his finger at me and orders me to get dressed at once.

Mr. Shapira tries to protest. "He's only a boy. This is inhuman!" He pulls on his trousers so he can come with me.

The officer tells him to shut up and begins cursing in Russian, using very bad words. The bad words flow out of him, as if he's an expert in cursing and wants to show off his skills.

"Silence, you miserable &!#*% cur, or I'll arrest you, too," he bellows.

Mr. Shapira steps back, though I can see how ashamed he is. I wish I could transmit a message to him telepathically. I want to tell him it's all right. The last thing I want is to get him and his family into trouble.

I try to dress as fast as I can, but I'm shivering with fear. If only Aunt Dora or my mother were here. Or, better still, Comrade Martha. She'd be able to explain to the soldiers that I'm a Pioneer, and I even won a revolutionary prize.

. I slip on my jacket and the soldiers lead me out of the house. I thought it was the middle of the night, but in fact it's early morning, and the first rays of light are spreading across the sky. A wagon hitched to two horses stands waiting for us on the road. The driver, whose face is half-hidden by his collar and hat, seems to be asleep.

As the cursing officer shoves me up onto the wagon, I realize he's a bit drunk. I can smell the alcohol on his breath. The other three officers just look bored.

The driver jerks awake and the cart lurches forward. My brain is going crazy with fear, but at least I'm not crying. And the reason I'm not crying is that all along the road people are opening their windows and doors to look at me, and I can tell they're astonished to see a boy under arrest, surrounded by four soldiers armed with rifles and bayonets. Their sympathetic faces and kind smiles give me hope, though no one dares to wave.

I'm shivering, but whether with cold or fright, I can't tell, because it's the first week of June, but it's still freezing out. I didn't have time to put on an undershirt or sweater. All I have under my jacket is my school shirt.

The police station, courthouse and jail are all in one building — the one where Papa was held for eight months. The drunk officer lifts me off the wagon. He marches me through the front door and down a narrow hallway. Then he pushes me into a cell and locks the door.

The cell is small and cold, and the cement walls look as if they have leprosy. The only furniture is a wooden platform covered by a thin, dirty mat, and the whole place smells like a mixture of horse pee, pig poop and dog vomit. It hurts my head to breathe in.

At least I can see into the hallway through the bars of the inside wall. I can hear people talking, and I can see them when they pass by. Maybe if I push my head against the bars and breathe the air outside the cell, I can escape the nauseating smell.

But as soon as I position my nose between two bars, I begin to cry uncontrollably, and though I'm trying not to make any sounds, my eyes are streaming.

All this time I imagined Papa in a nice warm room, talking and playing cards with his friends, sleeping on a real bed. But what if he was in this cell, or one exactly like it? Sleeping on a filthy mat, freezing, hungry, alone.

Crying makes my nose run, and I was too rushed when I got dressed to remember my handkerchief. I push my hand into my trouser pocket, not expecting to find anything. But somehow, in spite of all the confusion, Mrs. Shapira managed to slip in a clean handkerchief! I can hardly believe my luck.

I pull out the big light-blue handkerchief and blow my nose. The smell of sunshine and soap calms me down. Who would have thought a little piece of cloth could be such a lifesaver!

A story Comrade Martha told us comes back to me. When Lenin was in prison for his revolutionary activities, he communicated with the outside world by making a little inkpot out of bread and filling it with milk. He wrote secret instructions in the margins of books with milk. The writing could only be seen if you held the page up to a lamp.

I wouldn't mind some bread and milk. I'd gobble them up. I haven't had any breakfast and I'm starving.

But I'm feeling a little less scared now. After all, what can they do to me? Kids don't go to jail. And anyhow, Stalin loves children. I'm still in the dark about why I'm here, but all of a sudden I feel certain that the mix-up will be sorted out any minute, and that by tonight I'll be back at the Shapiras', eating supper with the family and playing "here comes the airplane" with Mitzi.

7

A Secret Message

"Stop lying!" the officer on the other side of the desk roars at me.

He's the ugliest man I've ever seen. He looks as if his head is made out of clay, and the person making the head was a four-year-old who just poked three holes for eyes and a mouth and piled on extra clay for a nose.

"You have three seconds to tell me where your mother is hiding!" he shouts. Then, switching to a quiet, threatening voice, he hisses, "When people don't cooperate, we lock them up in a cellar with rats. Is that what you want? Rats gnawing at your fingers and toes? Those rats are as big as cats."

I'm so petrified I begin to stutter. I'm also shaking from head to toe. I wonder if I'm having some kind of seizure.

The worst part is how much he hates me. I've never been hated before. At least, not specifically.

Mrs. Bubu hated me, but she hated everyone. Same with the Iron Guard. It wasn't personal.

But this man hates *me*, Natt Silver. It's the worst feeling in the world.

And for what? I truly, honestly, don't have a clue where my mother is. Why don't they believe me?

I'm blubbering again. "I'm a P-pioneer," I say. "I t-took an oath to love … to love and cherish my mother … my motherland." *Oh, no*, I think. *I hope he realizes that I'm just having trouble speaking, that I wasn't putting my mother ahead of my motherland.* "I even won a rev-revolutionary prize from Comrade Martha. Really, sir, I g-give you my word of honor that I don't know where she is."

"Pioneer!" he sneers and begins to laugh. "You, a Pioneer? You're the son of an Enemy of the People *and* a liar. That's what you are. And you're going to rot in the rat cellar until you tell me the truth."

My last bit of hope drains away. If I'm not a Pioneer, then I'm nothing, as far as they're concerned.

"I d-don't live with her during the week," I try to explain. "I only see her at weekends, at my … at my aunt's."

"I want a list of every single one of your relatives. And their addresses. Pronto!"

I do my best to remember the names of all my relatives and where they live, and as he writes down the information, he checks it against another piece of paper. He looks extremely angry every time he checks the paper. It makes him furious that I'm not providing him with any new information.

"What about Chernovitsy? Who are your relatives there?" he barks.

I'm concentrating so hard on trying to breathe that for a second my brain stops working and I forget that Czernowitz is Chernovitsy in Russian. Luckily, the blackout only lasts a second.

"I have an aunt there, Clara Geller," I say. "Clara and Hayim Geller." Clara and Hayim also have two children, Suzy and Hugo, but he doesn't need to know that.

"Geller!" He checks his list and snorts with satisfaction. I've finally given him a name he doesn't have on his list. "Address!" he blares out.

"I c-can't remember the exact number but it's f-four blocks from Theatre Square ..."

At that instant, like an angel who's been sent to protect me, a guard I haven't seen before enters the room and takes me away from the clay monster.

"I need a toilet," I tell him. He's younger than the other guards, and he looks at me when I speak. He reminds me a little of Max's brother Michael, with his dark, thoughtful eyes.

At first he hesitates. Then, making sure that the coast is clear, he escorts me to a little room with a sink and a flush toilet, like the one in Aunt Frieda's apartment. On the door there's a sign that says STAFF ONLY. I'm sure he's not allowed to let me use it, but he's doing it anyhow.

Maybe he's the same guard who told my mother when Papa would be looking out of the window.

The first thing I do is drink from the tap. I don't even care if the water is clean. I have to drink or I'll pass out. I wish I could spend more than a few minutes here, but I know I have to come out as quickly as possible. I don't want to get the guard in trouble.

Back in the cell, I sit on the plank, hold the handkerchief over my nose and shut my eyes. I have to find a way to calm down so I can breathe again. I try to think about something else. Something good. Our pear tree, for example. Olek and Papa built wood benches around the tree when I was little, and on summer evenings we all sat on the benches drinking lemonade and eating biscuits. Zoomie would shuffle from person to person hoping for crumbs, and her begging eyes always sent us into fits of laughter.

I'd do anything to have Zoomie here now, with her long warm fur under my fingers and her happy, drooling tongue on my face.

My breathing eventually returns to normal, but now my entire body is aching. I don't dare lie down on the filthy mat. I'm sure it's crawling with bugs. I'm cold and hungry and every bone in my body hurts.

Suddenly the most horrific thought of my life comes to me.

What if by giving the clay man the names of Clara and Hayim I've somehow betrayed them? What if because of me they get arrested, and their children are left all alone?

What have I done? If I'd thought of it before, I wouldn't have said a word, but it never even crossed my mind.

But what sort of trouble could Clara and Hayim be in? The clay man wants to find my mother, and he only asked for their names in case she's hiding there.

But what if she *is* hiding there? What if Clara and Hayim get sent to the Gulag for hiding my mother, and all because of me and my big mouth!

As if confirming my worst fears, the drunk, cursing officer who shoved me on the wagon storms into the cell, grabs my arm and pulls me out of the building. He isn't cursing now. He shoves me into the back of an open command car without a word. Then he climbs into the driver's seat and sits there absolutely motionless, like a toy soldier. His eyes are half shut and he doesn't even seem to be blinking.

Where are we going? What's happening? Are we going to look for Clara and Hayim?

I feel sick. Not only did I reveal their names, I'm now going to help the clay man find them.

The car doesn't have a roof, and I try to focus on the clean air and the blue summer sky. Judging by the position of the sun, it's around noon. I suddenly remember a song my mother sang to me when I was very little.

All the birds are here already,
Making music with their songs.
Whistling, chirping, trilling,
Urging spring along.
Birds, whose calls ring in our hearts,
We want to be happy, too.
We want to play and jump and laugh,
Like you.

A silly baby song, but it makes me miss my mother so much it's as if my heart has turned into a sponge and someone is wringing it.

I'm about to start crying again, but just then the young guard, the one who let me use the officers' facilities, joins me in the back of the command car. I feel better with him by my side. I shut my eyes and pretend he's Michael.

The driver is ready to go, but we have to wait for the ugly man. By now I know that he's the chief of police.

It's my first time in an open car, and I'm scared I'll tip over if we go fast, because there aren't any sides.

Eventually the chief comes huffing and puffing toward the car. He throws himself on the seat next to the driver, turns his ugly face around and snarls, "So. We'll soon see how much of a liar you are. We're going to pay your aunt in Chernovitsy a visit."

I was right! We're going to look for Clara and Hayim. The chief's voice convinces me that I've done the worst possible thing a human being can do. I betrayed my own family.

This time I can't hold back. Tears begin to trickle down my cheeks.

But suddenly the young guard sitting next to me gives my arm a quick, friendly nudge. I turn to him hopefully. His arms are crossed across his chest and he's looking straight ahead.

I understand. He wanted to send me a secret message, and he did.

And he must know. He must know whether I've betrayed Clara and Hayim or not. Maybe everything will be okay, especially if my mother isn't hiding there, and I don't think she is. She wouldn't choose such an obvious place. She's way too clever.

The car speeds down the road. A sweet scent of wildflowers fills the air, and the wind tickles my scalp. I'm no longer afraid of falling out because there's a bar to hold on to. If only it was my father driving, and we were all going on a picnic!

We reach the outer suburbs of the city in less

than an hour. It takes four to six hours by horse and cart.

The streets of Czernowitz are full of people, and the electric tram chugs slowly up the main street. Occasionally someone glances in our direction, then quickly looks away. They must be wondering what a kid is doing in a command car, but they don't want to call attention to themselves by staring. Over half the city's population is Jewish, and Max says Jews are getting more and more nervous about the war.

We pass the park where I tried to roller skate when I was eight, and the little theater where Mama and Papa took me to see a musical, *The Threepenny Opera*. The Romanian government wasn't too happy about plays in German, so the theater was a bit of a secret.

The most beautiful woman I'd ever seen, with red hair down to her waist, played Pirate Jenny. Pirate Jenny isn't really a pirate. She's just a downtrodden maid who likes to imagine she's a pirate.

For weeks after I saw the play I hummed her song about the ship with fifty cannons.

I think of the song now, especially the part where she imagines the pirates chaining up the men who bossed her around, and asking her, "Which one should we kill?" *Welchen sollen wir töten!*

We're moving at a snail's pace, stuck behind a horse and cart and other vehicles, including command cars like ours, filled with soldiers.

The chief turns to me and barks, "The exact address! Now!"

I tell the driver how to get to Aunt Clara's street, but for the life of me I can't remember the number of the apartment house.

"Don't play the fool," the chief growls at me. "I know all your tricks!"

"I'll … I'll recognize the house when I see it," I say. If only he'd stop shouting at me!

"You'd better, if you know what's good for you," he hisses, and he curls his fingers into a fist.

The traffic jam clears and a few minutes later we reach my aunt's street.

My heart sinks. All the buildings look the same, with their identical rows of decorated windows. What will happen now?

Then, as if stepping out from the crowd to help me, there it is. Aunt Clara's door! I recognize the curved glass panes and the engraving that looks like Hercule Poirot's moustache over the arch.

"There — that's the one!" I cry out. "She's on the first floor. Apartment Five." For a second I get all excited, thinking I'll see my aunt, and forgetting that I'm still not sure if she's in trouble because I blabbed.

But of course I won't be seeing her. When I realize that there's no chance at all, I begin to sob in great big gasps, but luckily the chief of police and the driver are already striding to the door.

"I'm missing school," I tell the guard beside me. As usual, my sobs turn to hiccups as I try to hold them in. "And our teacher — *hic* — is reading us *War and* — *hic* — *Peace*."

At first he doesn't answer. He looks to the left and to the right, then over his shoulder. Then he says, under his breath, "Your Russian is very good."

"I came first — *hic* — in Russian," I blurt out stupidly.

He nods, and I decide to take the plunge and ask about Papa. It's my only chance. "Did you know my father?

He nods again. I can tell he's not supposed to be talking about it.

"Was he — *hic* — in the same cell as me?"

"The permanent prisoners are in the back," he says, barely moving his lips. "You're in the temporary cell. Now, no more conversation, please."

And to my surprise he starts singing a Russian song, maybe to stop me from speaking, or to stop himself. It's a sad melody, but for some reason a sad song can make you feel less sad.

I also like the sound of the word *temporary*. I'm in the temporary cell. That means I won't be staying long.

And the guard knew what I was asking. He knew I was asking if Papa's cell was as awful as mine. And his answer is no.

I'm so grateful and relieved I want to hug him. Maybe one day, after the war, I will.

The driver and the chief come charging out of the building. Alone! They haven't arrested anyone!

I look up at the window. And there she is! Aunt Clara leans out and blows me a kiss. She also waves an empty bowl. I think she's trying to say that she would have sent me a snack if she could. Or that next time I come there will be a bowl of treats waiting for me.

I force a smile, but I don't dare wave back.

"What do you think you're doing!" the chief roars at me, and I nearly jump out of my skin. "You think this is some kind of joke? Your mother has committed an act of treason!"

I almost faint when he says that. Everyone knows that treason is punishable by death.

But the friendly guard nudges me again. This time the nudge means *Don't take him seriously.*

I'm ready to give that guard everything I have for the rest of my life.

I'm back in my cell for only a few minutes when I hear Aunt Dora's voice! She's begging to be allowed to give me a coat. It's mid-afternoon, I still haven't had anything to eat, and I'm exhausted in every possible way — my body, my heart, my brain, my soul.

By some miracle, the chief isn't here. He never would have agreed, but his replacement takes the coat and a few minutes after Dora leaves, a woman in uniform brings it to me.

It's my heavy winter coat. I check the pockets. Nothing.

Then I remember the secret pocket in the lining. It would have been easy to find that pocket if anyone had checked, but it seems no one bothered.

And that is very, very lucky, because there's a chocolate bar hidden inside!

I've never been so glad to see a chocolate bar in my life. And chocolate has never tasted so good. I gobble it down, keeping my back to the hallway in case someone passes by.

Once I've finished, it occurs to me that the wrapping, when I undid it, was loose. I take another look and see that there's a note scrawled on the inside: *Don't worry, your mother is coming to pick you up.* It isn't signed, just in case.

I quickly tear the wrapping into small pieces and scrape them into the dirty cement floor with my shoes, until they blend in with the black sludge.

Then I wipe my mouth with the handkerchief.

I feel less alone now, thanks to Aunt Dora, the warm coat, the secret note, the chocolate — and the news that my mother is coming. Max won't believe his ears when I tell him the story. It's straight out of *The Three Musketeers*.

As soon as the chief of police returns, he orders the guards to bring me to his office for another interview. I've barely had a chance to sit down before he grabs his gun, leans across the desk and points it at my head.

"We've had enough of your lies." His voice is shaking with rage. "Tell me the truth, or I will pull the trigger!"

I freeze in terror.

If only I could tell him my mother is coming. But he'll want to know how I know, and that will only make things worse. In any case, I couldn't speak even if I wanted to. All I can do is pray that my mother shows up before he kills me.

I want to say something — anything. But as soon as I try to speak, I begin to choke and wheeze.

The chief of police drops the gun in disgust and orders the woman guard who gave me the coat to throw me back in the cell. Even though the gun is no longer pointed at me, I can't move. My legs collapse under me when I try to stand, and the guard has to place her hands under my armpits and slide me along the floor like a rag doll.

Your mother is coming. Your mother is coming. I repeat the secret message over and over until gradually, bit by bit, I revive.

I tell myself the gun probably wasn't even loaded. But at the same time I have a chilling suspicion that the chief of police really did want to kill me. And would have if he could.

8

My Mother Puts on a Show

I never knew my mother could act. But as it turns out, she's a fantastic actress.

I'm huddled inside my coat, my entire body aching from being scrunched up in one position, when I think I hear her voice. I jump up and throw myself against the cell bars.

Yes, it's definitely Mama, though there's something strange about the way she's talking. For one thing, her voice is a lot louder than usual, as if she's acting in a play. A comedy.

And because it's a comedy, she's laughing. Laughing with the chief of police!

My mother and the chief come waltzing down the hallway. They're both smiling and chatting as if they're the best of friends. Mama is wearing bright red lipstick and she's wrapped a silk perfumed kerchief — white with yellow flowers — around her neck. She's also got on her special-occasion white gloves, and she's pinned her hair up with a comb.

"Natt, my darling," she says when she sees me. "What a silly mistake. They thought I was hiding, when I was simply visiting an old friend whose mother is ill. And this nice gentleman told me what a good boy you've been, and how cooperative. I'm so proud of you."

The chief of police has a big smirk on his ugly clay face.

I get what my mother is doing. She's flattering the chief and he's falling for it. He probably doesn't get a lot of women trying to charm him.

The female guard unlocks the cell, and my mother does her best to act casual when she sees me. I play along.

"Thank you, sir," I say to the man who, a few hours ago, held a gun to my head, and who still hasn't given me a bite to eat. "You've been very kind."

It seems I'm discovering some hidden acting talents myself.

"My dear lady, I'm going to do you a favor," the chief says, puffing his chest out. "Because you've come here on your own, and because your son has been so cooperative, I'm going to give you the entire night to pack. And I'm going to trust you to wait for us tomorrow morning at six sharp. That gives you ..." He checks his gold watch. "Sixteen hours."

"You're too kind. I will never forget you." My mother flashes her brightest smile. "I will, of course, be there. I want to contribute to the Revolution in any way I can."

Aunt Dora's house is a sultan's palace after my day in prison. As soon as we're safely indoors, everyone begins fussing over me. Aunt Dora tells me there's a hot bath and a meal waiting for me. They all seem to be feeling guilty, especially Mama, even though none of it was their fault.

I'm torn between washing and eating. I'm famished, but I'm also dying to get rid of the putrid prison smell that seems to be clinging to me. I gulp down a glass of milk to tide me over and jump into the tin tub for a quick bath and shampoo.

Ten minutes later I'm at the kitchen table, trying not to tear into the delicious meal that Aunt Dora has prepared for me.

"You poor darling," she says. "Did you get my note?"

I nod. "And the chocolate. Thank you! And Mrs. Shapira stuck a handkerchief in my pocket. And the nice guard took me to the officers' toilet. He knows Papa. And I drove in a command car all the way to Aunt Clara's. She waved at me from the window."

I decide not to say anything about the gun or the rat cellar.

Mama and Aunt Dora laugh with relief.

Then they explain about the quota. "All the chief cares about is filling his quota."

"What's a quota?" I ask, shoveling rice into my mouth.

My aunt slams her knife into a loaf of bread. She doesn't want to lose her temper, so she's letting it out on the bread.

"It's a specific number a person has to reach," she says. "In this case, the quota is the number of people who need to be arrested. If the chief of police doesn't fill his quota, he could be sent to the Gulag himself. To them, we're just two more people to tick off the list."

"That doesn't make s …" But the last word is lost inside a great big yawn.

"Poor Natty, you're exhausted … he's exhausted, poor thing!" my mother and aunt cry out together.

"The chief of police liked you," I say. What I want to say is *Thank you* and *You were fantastic* and *I'm proud of you* and *We tricked that nincompoop,* but somehow, I can't get those words out.

"Yes, I deserve an acting award," my mother replies. "If he'd thought I was hiding, I'd be finished. And we really *are* lucky that we have time to pack." She looks down at her plate and sighs. "I'm not in the least bit hungry, but who knows when we'll eat again."

"Yes, eat, *mama'le*," Dora says. "I'll go and find the biggest suitcases we have." I've never heard Dora use the Yiddish word *mama'le* before.

"So where exactly did you say we were going?" I try to sound casual, as if the information just slipped my mind, because I have a feeling that I'm expected to know by this point.

"Didn't I say? We're off to Siberia! Lots of people live in Siberia of their own free will," my mother adds quickly. "There are forests and lakes, and in some places you can even swim at the beach in summer. And best of all, we'll be moving east, away from the fighting … It's going to be a real adventure."

My eyes begin to droop. Pushing my plate aside, I let my head flop down on my arms. Images of Siberian beaches fade into the blackout of a deep, dreamless sleep.

"Wake up, lazybones!"

I'm dreaming that Max is shouting in my ear, trying to wake me up.

Except that it's not a dream. Max really *is* shouting in my ear.

I open my eyes and see him standing right there next to me, clutching his schoolbag in his arms.

Where am I? What is Max doing here?

I sit up. I'm at Aunt Dora's, of course. They must

have carried me from the table to the sofa. I check the clock. Ten past three. It's dark outside, so it must be three at night.

Why is Max here in the middle of the night?

"I brought you some things for your trip," Max says. His eyes are wet and the tip of his nose is red.

"I was in jail," I tell him. "Real jail, Max. With bars! And the chief of police put a gun to my head. He said he'd shoot if I didn't tell him where my mother was, or put me in a cellar with rats. But don't tell anyone … How did you get here?"

Max dumps his schoolbag on the floor, sinks into the corner of the sofa and tucks his legs under him. He looks smaller than ever, curled up against the arm cushions.

"I heard you were arrested," he says. His voice sounds small, too. He's probably still half-asleep. "A kid in jail, what next? But — a real gun?"

"Well, I don't think it was loaded. He just wanted to fill his quota." Quota. It's as if I've known the word forever. Like Gulag. "It was straight out of *The Three Musketeers*. Though not really. It's different when it's real."

The room is chilly, and Max shivers.

"I brought you some things to take in your schoolbag," he says again. "Dad left all sorts of medicines behind. They might come in useful."

"How did you get here?"

"Your uncle came round to fetch me. He thought I'd want to say goodbye."

"Where is everyone?" I ask.

"Your mother is sleeping. You aunt and uncle are upstairs, probably packing."

Packing. That's right, we're going to Siberia, just like Papa.

"My mother says there are beaches in Siberia," I tell him. "You can swim in the summer."

Max nods. "It's a big area, so everything depends on where you end up. It's good you're going now, in June." He reaches over for his schoolbag and unbuckles it. There's a picture of Lenin glued to the inside flap, but the paper's a bit scuffed, and part of Lenin's face is rubbed out.

"Poor Lenin," I say. "Oh, that's another thing. I'm no longer a Pioneer."

"That whole Pioneer thing is stupid," Max says fiercely. "What does it even mean? Who cares? It's just a way to make us believe we're part of it. If Stalin —" The anger fizzles out of him. "Don't listen to me," he says with a sigh. "But remember what I told you. Don't say anything bad about Stalin or the Party or anything else, to anyone. I heard someone was sent to a gulag for cracking a joke about the Kremlin. Are you listening, Natt? I'm serious."

I don't want to think about any of that now, but I nod to make him happy.

Max empties the contents of his schoolbag on the blanket. "Tell me if there's something else you want," he says. "There's lots of time. I can run home and get it for you."

"Wow, Max. This is a lot of stuff." I feel like an explorer putting together my gear for the long journey.

Max has brought:

5 pencils and a brass pencil sharpener
envelopes
a bottle of iodine
sulfa and Aspirin pills
a tin of Camphor Balm for Man or Beast
(*for the relief of neuralgia, toothache, strains, sprains, bruises, insect bites and muscular rheumatic pains*)
bandages and tiny scissors to cut them
a pair of socks (knit by Rita and Raya)
two bars of soap
candles and matches
my stardust marble (he's been keeping the marbles at his place)
a sliding number puzzle (fifteen numbers)
cards and our tiny booklet of card-game rules
chocolate wafers
shoelaces
a fake Musketeer moustache

"A moustache?" I ask, laughing.

Max smiles. "You never know when you'll need a disguise. Also, this is from my mother." He takes a matchbox out of his pocket. Inside, wrapped in gauze, is a gold ring.

"Hide it somewhere safe," he says. "Like in a ball of wool."

"I can't take this." I hand the matchbox back to him. "You're going to need it to buy train tickets to Switzerland. We have enough money. It's sewn into our coats."

With a polite cough Aunt Dora announces her entrance. She's carrying a tray of tea and what looks like a box of chocolates.

"Max, how are you?" she says. "Sorry we woke you. We guessed you'd want to say goodbye. I've been saving these chocolates for a special occasion, and that occasion has arrived."

I hope for Max's sake that the chocolates are filled with marzipan.

"Thanks, Aunt Dora," I say. "Look at what Max brought."

"That's very kind of you, dear. I'm sure it will all come in handy." Then she bursts into tears, and to my horror, she leaps over to the sofa and clasps me to her! I've never been so humiliated in my life.

I do my best to squirm out of her grip. On top of everything else, she's squishing me right against her bosomy chest!

"I'm sorry," she says, realizing too late that she's crossed the line of normal human behavior. "I'll miss you."

"We'll write," I say, a bit ashamed of how rude I was. I kind of pushed her away, but I needed to breathe.

"Yes …" she says. "Now, is there anything special you want me to pack, Natt?"

"The fur hat, please," I say, remembering the hat Max gave me.

"Yes, I packed every warm thing we have. And my best mohair blanket. It's wonderfully light. And they said to pack food, too. I'm afraid you can hardly lift the suitcases now."

I don't suppose I'll be able to say goodbye to the Shapiras. Or anyone else.

It's still pitch-black outside.

It's as if I'm taking part in a secret mission.

I await instructions!

THREE
MINUS A COUNTRY

1941
SUMMER

1

Exile

We've been ready since 6:00 a.m. with two suitcases, a bundle of pillows, two quilts tied up in a sheet, my schoolbag and a knapsack stuffed with food.

We've also filled one of Papa's old burlap grain bags, the kind with a drawstring on top. The bag is filled with extra things we're not sure we'll be allowed to take. We're planning to wear our boots and our winter coats on top of our spring coats.

It's nearly noon and no one has come for us. We've extended our breakfast for so long that it's turned into lunch.

"Maybe they've forgotten about us," my mother says hopefully.

Max is still here. He's making a list of all the things we're going to do when I get back from Siberia. Slide down a mountain on a bobsled, carve a Musketeer chess set, invent a remote-control airplane, explore the Amazon.

I'm making a list, too. I'm listing all the things I used to have in my room, which I plan to recover or replace when the war is over. Maybe the bits that don't have any value, like my snake skins and so on, really are in storage somewhere. The rest were probably sold.

I'm biting into my sixth piece of buttered toast when there's a knock on the door.

They're here.

Dora opens the door, and a soldier with a rifle slung over his shoulder and a clipboard in his hands enters the house.

"Sophia Silver, Nathan Silver," he recites in a monotone, consulting his clipboard.

"Yes, that's us," my mother says, giving him her sunniest smile. "Thank you for not forgetting us."

How does she do it? Five minutes ago she was wiping away tears.

He points to Max and asks me, "Is that your brother?"

And Max, to everyone's shock, says, "Yes, I'm his brother."

He wants to come with me to Siberia!

"He's just joking," I tell the soldier.

The soldier checks his paper. "I don't have your name here," he tells Max, "but if you're his brother, you had better come along."

At that exact second, Max's mother shows up, a little out of breath. When she grasps what has just happened, she begins to shriek hysterically, "That's my son! Max Zwecker! Zwecker, Zwecker! My husband is in Switzerland — Dr. Emil Zwecker! I have three sons and two daughters! My husband is a doctor!"

I've never heard Max's mother raise her voice above a soft murmur. But now she's shrieking so loudly, and at such a high pitch, that my ears are ringing. She looks absolutely terrified and her face is as white as a sheet. She's clutching Max even more fiercely than Dora clutched me. I feel for him.

The soldier shrugs. He doesn't care.

I'm glad it's been decided. On the one hand, it would be fantastically great to have Max with me on the journey. Maximus and Natius, off on an adventure! On the other hand, I'd feel awful taking him away from his family, especially if there's still a chance they'll be joining his father. And seeing Max's mother in hysterics makes it clear to everyone, including me, that she'd rather die than be parted from Max.

Max is crying now. Really blubbering. I haven't seen him cry since we got lost in the forest in first grade, and it makes me feel terrible. I want to do something about it, but I can't think what.

"Can we bring this?" Mama points to the large burlap bag and produces another glowing smile, as if the prince at a ball has just asked her to dance.

The soldier shrugs. "As long as you can carry it, and as long as it doesn't slow down the horses."

"So kind, so kind," my mother says as we step outside. Max follows us, still sobbing but doing his best to stop.

I blink in the bright sunlight. And then I blink again, this time not because of the light, but because I can't believe what I'm seeing.

The street is lined with every type of one-horse and two-horse cart and wagon, each one jam-packed with townspeople, old and young and in between. The procession is so long I can't even see where it ends.

Are all these people leaving with us? I thought we'd be on our own. But it seems we're part of a mass exodus.

This expedition suddenly feels a lot less like an adventure, and more like we're being banished.

Yes, that's the word. Banished. We're being banished from our home. Forced to leave, whether we want to or not.

There's something else, too. I can't say why, but I assumed we'd be back in a few weeks.

But now it looks as if something much more serious is going on.

How long will we be gone? Months? A whole year?

Max vanishes inside the house, probably to look for a handkerchief, and by the time he returns we're already on the wagon with our bags, and the wagon is moving. All we can do is wave one last time and promise to write.

"Aren't we lucky," my mother says. "They picked us up last, we're in the least crowded wagon *and* they let us keep the extra bag." She whispers in my ear, "I have a surprise in the bag. I'll show you later."

A few mounted soldiers ride alongside the wagons. People come out of their houses to watch and wave and shout "Good luck!" in their various languages. I'm reminded of my language game from long ago. Finally, I've found a phrase that's different in all six languages. Good luck.

Suddenly someone bolts out from the crowd and begins running after our wagon.

It's Comrade Minsky!

Luckily, we're moving very slowly, and then our procession stops altogether. Comrade Minsky soon catches up with us. He hands one of the passengers a package and points to me.

The passenger, an old man with a white beard, passes me the package.

It's two old books with worn paper covers, tied together with string and more string. I move the string aside so I can see the title, and I discover that I'm holding Part One and Part Two of *War and Peace*!

I look up to thank Comrade Minsky, but I can't see him anywhere. He's disappeared into the crowd. But that's okay. He knows I'd thank him if I could.

The horses resume their relaxed pace, and then, just as our wagon passes our old house, they halt again.

It's a coincidence, of course, but it's as if the entire procession stopped at this exact spot so we could say goodbye to our house.

The guards gather on the street. They're checking their papers and having a loud discussion right in front of our old door, which now has a big Russian sign over it: *GOSUDARSTVENNY BANK*.

I want to jump out of the wagon, dash to the house, mount Lightning III and gallop up and down the veranda that runs along the sides and back of the house.

Well, maybe I'm getting too old to ride an imaginary horse, but I still love that veranda. When I was five I jumped from the railing to see what it felt like to fly to Neverland. I fell flat on my face and broke my finger. When the doctor asked me how it happened, I said, "Peter Pan broke my finger." Everyone burst out laughing, and my silly answer became a family joke. *Peter Pan brach mir den Finger.*

I wonder if the back garden looks the same now. I'd give anything to take a peek. Why didn't I think to do that when it was still possible?

I also wonder what became of our two beautiful horses, Samson and Delilah. Papa and I used to hitch them to the wagon and travel down country roads to the quarries to look at the work being done there, or to farms to buy grain. Along the way, I'd pick up treasures for my nature collection.

Do the horses miss us? I hope they found a good home. Or maybe Olek is looking after them at his place.

From where I'm sitting I can see our summer kitchen, our laundry house and a corner of Papa's brick warehouse. Max and I were crazy about the warehouse. It was like having our own private amusement park. On the upper floor there were all these little compartments filled with wheat, barley, oats, rye, sunflower seeds, pumpkin seeds and all kinds of beans and nuts. Each compartment had a hatch in the floor with a chute for sliding the grains down when it was time to ship them. We used to take off our shoes, jump into a bin and let ourselves sink into the grain while stuffing ourselves stupid with pumpkin seeds and pretending an evil sorcerer had kidnapped us.

Sometimes Lucy joined us and used her ingenuity to outwit the sorcerer.

Lucy ... I didn't have a chance to say goodbye to her. I already miss the smell of her scented soap and the way she holds her playing cards right up to her nose like a fan.

I steal a glance at Mama. She's staring at the house with a puzzled expression on her face, as if she can't understand how her life could have changed so much.

When she sees me looking at her, her frown changes instantly into a smile. She takes my hand

and exclaims, "How lucky that we have a chance to say goodbye to our house!"

Can she really mean it? Does she really think we're lucky to be faced with our old house, a house that is no longer ours?

All at once, I know the answer. If Max were here he'd say I was having a Flash of Genius. But it doesn't take a genius to see what's going on.

Mama is not only putting on an act for the people in charge. She's also putting on an act for me. She doesn't want me to be scared, so she's pretending that everything is fine and dandy.

And now I have to pretend, too, because if I let on that I'm unhappy, she'll be even more upset than she is already.

So she's pretending and I'm pretending. Neither of us can say what we really feel about the old house, the wooden seat around the pear tree, Zoomie, the warehouse, Samson and Delilah. Neither of us can say or show what we feel about Papa being sent to Siberia and the two of us following him — and not even to the same place, as far as we know.

I nod my head and say quietly, "You're right, Mama. It is lucky. Remember 'Peter Pan broke my finger'?"

Well, that's exactly the right thing to bring up, because she bursts out laughing and repeats the sentence over and over, *Peter Pan brach mir den Finger, Peter Pan brach mir den Finger.*

She's starting to sound a bit insane, but that's okay. The war is insane.

On the street, the officers' discussion is getting more and more heated. They're standing only a few feet from us, and everyone on our wagon can hear their conversation. It's about how many of us there are.

Their list says 138, and they've ticked off every name, but when they count us, they come up with 137.

They can't figure it out. No matter how many times they count us, the total comes to 137: *sto tridtsad sem*. They repeat the number over and over.

It must be that quota thing. They need 138 people and they'll be in trouble if they only have 137.

Suddenly one of the soldiers notices something. I recognize him. He's the Jewish soldier who spoke to us in Yiddish when the Russians first came to town. I remember how he told us that everything would be fine.

Anyhow, he notices that a woman called Anna Fisher is listed twice.

Now they're really frantic. Are there two women called Anna Fisher, or has Anna Fisher been listed twice by accident? To add to the confusion, the spelling of the two Anna Fishers on the list is not exactly the same. So now they're questioning a woman by the name of Anna Fisher, who is sitting in the wagon next to us, about how she spells her name. Fisher or Fischer?

The woman turns out to be the mother of one of the men who was arrested with Papa. She's old and deaf and a little confused, and the soldiers have to shout. They ask others in the wagon to translate for them, and soon everyone is shouting at this poor old woman, including three little kids.

Then a baby starts to cry. No one even knew this baby was there, because it's a newborn who is being fed under a big cloak.

The officers don't know what to do. They're obviously terrified of the quota.

"Is the baby listed?" the Jewish soldier thinks to ask.

After some more back-and-forth discussion, it turns out that the baby is not on the list because she was born after the list was put together. And she wasn't counted today because she was hidden by her mother's cloak.

So they rename the baby Anna Fischer. Problem solved. They now have 138 people.

"From now on, your baby is called Anna Fischer," they tell the baby's mother. "Do you understand?"

The mother nods quickly, her eyes wide with fear. I think she was scared they'd take her baby away from her.

The ghost of a smile appears on Mama's face. And on the faces of a few other people on our wagon. They're trying not to look at each other in case they give themselves away by laughing out loud.

I get it. They know the real Anna Fischer, and they're pleased that we've managed to trick the NKVD. Anna Fischer has escaped, and a baby has taken her place.

Now that we're all accounted for, the soldiers give orders to the drivers to ride on to Czernowitz. The old man who handed me Comrade Minsky's package says, "And from there to Siberia, where we can contribute to the great enterprise of building this wonderful socialist society."

I'm pretty sure he's being sarcastic, though he says it with a straight face.

Maybe he believes it. I don't think anyone else does. Even if they support equality, I don't think anyone believes this trip is what Marx or Lenin had in mind. It's one hundred percent Stalin.

Who, it turns out, does not like kids after all.

Or, judging by these wagons, Jews or Poles or farmers or doctors or teachers or Ukrainians or journalists or priests — or probably anyone else on the planet other than himself.

2

The Fortune Teller

The horses walk at a relaxed pace, and the guards let us stop every hour or so to stretch our legs or answer the call of nature behind a tree. People sip water from metal canteens, but we're all saving our food for later. At one point an axle breaks and needs to be repaired.

While the wheel is being fixed, out of nowhere, a zillion birds appear in the sky. They're traveling in a flock, and they glide back and forth in fantastic geometric patterns. They remind me of my old kaleidoscope.

All of us, including the guards, stare up at the sky. It's as if the birds are putting on a show just for us.

And then they're gone. It's the end of the show.

When the wheel is fixed, we return to our wagons. After each stop, we have to be counted again. The soldiers need to check that no one has escaped. In the end, it takes us over six hours to get to Czernowitz. That's six times longer than it took in the command car.

We arrive at our destination — a big L-shaped high school two stories high, with long rows of windows peering down at us. It seems we'll be staying in the school gym for now.

Mama and I have a problem. We have too much stuff. I count the suitcases and bags: seven in all. Two suitcases, one bundle tied up in a sheet, one school-bag, one knapsack, Mama's shoulder bag and the grain bag with the surprise.

The soldiers help us unload, but after that we're on our own. We have no idea what to do.

Suddenly we hear someone calling, "Mrs. Silver? Natt? Over here!"

It's Irena, my music teacher's daughter, who's been studying to be a schoolteacher here in the city, and whose books Max and I used to borrow.

Irena weaves through the crowd to reach us. She's seventeen or eighteen, and very pretty, with big blue eyes and fluffy pale blonde hair and skin like a porcelain doll. Her sweet dimpled smile lights up her face.

"How terrific to see you here," she says. "I was visiting my mother's relatives last week, and when I came home, my parents were gone. Just like that — gone. All I can find out is that they've been arrested. I've asked everyone I can think of where they've been taken, but no luck so far. You wouldn't happen to know anything?"

My mother shakes her head. "I'm sorry, dear. I didn't even notice that they were gone. I've been so busy ..."

"Mother's Ukrainian, but Father as you know is Polish, and I heard they were deporting Poles. I've asked at the police station, at the army base, I've even been stopping soldiers on the street, but I can't get any answers. Someone thought they might be here, so … here I am. Voluntarily, if you can believe it!"

"I think you should go back," my mother suggests gently.

"But this is my only chance. I'm hoping to find them on one of the trains. Would you mind if I joined you?"

Even I'm wondering if that's a good idea, and I'm just a kid. Siberia is enormous. What are the odds of Irena finding her parents by boarding some random train that's headed who knows where?

"Of course, of course," my mother says, and I can see she's really happy, happier than she wants to let on, that Irena will be joining us.

"Are all these things yours?" Irena asks.

"Yes," my mother says with a small embarrassed laugh. "I wasn't sure how long we'd be gone."

"No, no, it's good that you brought as much as possible. Let me help you. My bags are already inside."

The three of us drag our luggage to the gym. I thought it would be only the 137 people from our town in the gym (plus Baby Anna), but there are at least double that number already inside.

How many people are leaving for Siberia? And what exactly are we all going to do once we get there?

We have to step over resting bodies and stretched-out legs as we walk. We wouldn't know what to do on our own, but Irena leads the way to one of the walls, where she's already set up a little corner for herself.

Once we're settled, I breathe a sigh of relief and look around. Kids are climbing the exercise ladders at the other end of the gym and swinging on ropes that hang from the rafters. I recognize some of the kids from my school.

"Go ahead," my mother urges. She's busy organizing our things. "Let me know if you get hungry."

I'm starving, but I don't want to miss out on the fun, so I join my friends. We invent games that take into account our limited space, such as who can do the most press-ups on the ladders or pass a ball with one hand without dropping it. The adults don't seem to mind, even when one boy loses his grip on the rope and comes crashing down on an entire family.

My stomach begins to growl. Lots of people are eating now, and the smell of olives and hard-boiled eggs fills the gym. I climb down from the ladder and thread my way through the maze of bodies until I reach Mama and Irena.

As soon as I plop down beside her, Mama says cheerfully, "What luck that Irena is here!"

It turns out that everyone likes Irena, and that means they tell her things. She circulates among the other deportees (that's what we're called, *deportees* — another new word), talks to the guards and returns loaded with information. No one will tell us where we're going or how long we'll be staying in the gym, but Irena has the lowdown on toilets, medicine, who is here, where they've come from, how to send a letter, how to buy extra food.

"The soldiers say we should buy food while we can, because on the trains there isn't going to be much."

I get the hint, and only eat two pieces of bread, though I could easily gobble down half a loaf.

Julian and Carl, two boys from home whose parents ran a print shop, signal for me to come over to their spot. As I move toward them, I hear a raspy voice calling out in Romanian, "Little boy, little boy!"

I stop in my tracks, but I don't see anyone.

"Here, here!"

I turn again, and this time I spot the fortune teller from the market. The one who told Lana she was going to live in a mansion in the United States.

She's about a million years old. I've never seen anyone this old. She was always partly hidden by veils, plus Max and I mostly saw her from the back when we were spying on her, and the tent was kind of dark, so I had no idea how wrinkled she was. She has a whole landscape of ravines and gullies carved on her face.

"Little boy, will you bring me some water?" She's sitting by herself, surrounded by people who aren't paying any attention to her. She only has one small bundle and she's leaning sideways on it. She seems to be wearing at least five dark-gray robes, one on top of the other.

"Water? Oh … of course," I tell her.

The soldiers at the door are in charge of water. They hand it out in a tin cup, which they dip into a barrel. You're supposed to drink it there and hand the cup back. Everyone's drinking from the same cup and the soldier's hand touches the water each time. I hope Mama, whose biggest fear is "dangerous microbes," doesn't pass out when she sees this arrangement.

"Can I please borrow the cup for a few minutes?" I ask. "I'll bring it back straight away, I promise. It's for that old lady there." I point, even though the soldier can't possibly tell who I'm pointing to. The gym is packed with old women.

The soldier agrees. It's a challenge to get the water back to the fortune teller without spilling, but I manage somehow.

She thanks me with a wrinkly grin and gulps all the water in one go but holds on to the empty cup. She wants me to stay a little longer.

"You're the boy who used to spy on me," she says.

My jaw drops. How can she possibly know it was me and Max giggling outside her tent? Maybe she really does have secret powers.

"Come, sit down for a minute. Yes, it was you and your little red-headed friend. What, did you think I couldn't hear you laughing? Sit, sit."

I do my best to find a few inches of floor.

"Let me read your palm," she offers, taking hold of my hand. Her fingers make me think of chicken feet.

In spite of the noise and her low, croaky voice, I have no trouble hearing her. It's actually a bit quieter now, because it's getting late and some of the kids are asleep. Some of the grown-ups, too.

"Oh, my," she says, studying my palm. "You're here with your mother?"

"Yes," I tell her. "My father was sent to the Gulag."

"Yes, yes," she says, trailing her bony finger along the lines on my hand. I have to admit that I'm curious to hear her predictions, even if they're just made up. "The three of you will survive, little boy. You will all be reunited at the end of the war. Many will die, but not you or your parents. I, for example, am going to die tonight."

I feel a little sick when she says that, and I shake my head. But she smiles and her eyes soften.

"Don't worry, precious. I'm nearly a hundred years

old, and this is a good place to die. You, too, will live to a very old age. But not here. In another country. Not in Europe."

"Canada?"

"Maybe, I'm not sure."

"Do you want more water?" I ask.

"No, no, kind boy. I'm fine now. Let me finish telling your fortune. You will find true love with a pretty girl. And your parents will live to have grandchildren. Many good people will help you along the way, but beware of a woman with red eyes. Remember — keep your secrets to yourself."

Now she's sounding like Max.

"Ah, you miss your little friend," she says. "And you miss a pretty little girl, too."

Lucy! I still have the note she gave me, the one with the heart. I keep it in the inside pocket of my coat. To be perfectly honest, the next day I gave her a note with an even bigger heart.

I nod. "How long until I go home?"

She bobs her head a few times, then folds my hand and returns it to my lap.

"You'll return when the war ends, but you'll have to be clever about it. Clever and sneaky. Don't be afraid. Be careful, but not afraid."

When the war ends. Well, no one knows when that's going to be. The Great War lasted four years and three months. But this war won't last anywhere near as long. They won't make the same mistakes they made last time.

"Go back to your mother, little man," she says. "Help her out."

She shuts her eyes. I remember my promise to return the cup, so I hurry back to the soldier.

"Was that your grandmother?" he asks. Even though he's being friendly, his face and eyes remain blank.

"No, she's a fortune teller. How long do you think we'll be here?"

"Why does everyone keep asking me that?" he says grumpily. "The fortune teller knows as much as I do. Why don't you ask *her*?"

"Sorry."

"Your Russian is good," he comments, but he doesn't sound or look impressed. He doesn't sound or look anything. He could be a robot. A slightly grumpy robot.

"I learned it at school. Our teacher started us on *War and Peace*. He gave me a copy to take with me."

The soldier's face lights up.

"Tolstoy — one of the greats," he says. It seems I've hit upon the magic words, because suddenly he's a whole different person. "Chekhov, Dostoevsky, Gorky, Pasternak, Pushkin. Remember that list for me. Can you remember it?"

I repeat the list, and he nods.

"I used to be an actor," he confides. "I acted in a Chekhov play once. *The Cherry Orchard.*"

"What part did you play?"

"A wimp." He laughs, and I'm hoping he'll tell me more, but just then a man drives into the court-yard with a whole cartload of food for sale, and our orderly group of sleepy deportees turns into a wild mob, clamoring to go outside and buy food.

"One at a time!" the former actor booms angrily. "There's enough for everyone. If you don't stop yelling and pushing, no one will be allowed out."

He's back to being a soldier.

3

Under Attack

The Nazis have invaded Russia! That means us, because we're part of Russia now.

Hitler promised Russia he wouldn't invade. That was the pact. But it was all a trick. Elias, my old Hebrew teacher, was right. Hitler never planned to keep his promise.

And I can actually tell Elias that he was right, because he's here, now, in the gym.

This morning the gym emptied out. The people who were here before us have been taken to a train heading for Siberia.

For a few hours we kids went crazy. We stole hats and threw them around. We even shouted Yiddish and Russian curses from the top of the climbing ropes. *May you turn into a lump of cheese and be snatched by a cat! May you walk backwards for the rest of your life and fall into outhouses!* The guards couldn't decide whether to shout at us or laugh.

But right after lunch — a bowl of disgusting soup which most people couldn't eat — hundreds of new people joined us. So now we're like sardines again. And it's begun to smell bad, too — partly because the toilets are broken and partly because none of us can wash ourselves or even brush our teeth properly. Ugh.

I'm playing cards with Julian and Carl when I spot Elias. He's one of the last to join us in the gym, and in fact I notice his four-year-old daughter, Shainie, first, because she's sitting on her father's shoulders. Her Shirley Temple curls bounce as he turns this way and that, looking for a place to settle. His wife, Cecilia, is holding on to his arm.

I call out to them, and in spite of the din, they hear me.

Elias is so happy to see me that he wraps his arms around me as if he were my father. In wartime, it seems, people can become parents on the spot.

"Cecilia, look who's here," Elias says. "My star pupil. Are you all right, Natt? Who are you here with?"

Cecilia gives me a hug, too, and Shainie giggles.

"I'm here with my mother," I tell them. "And Irena, the music teacher's daughter. Sorry about the smell," I add, as if this is my home and I'm the host. "The toilets are broken."

"Yes, yes." Elias bobs his head up and down. He's even more of a nervous wreck than when I last saw him. It's as if he's on a raft in the middle of the ocean, and he doesn't think anyone's going to rescue him.

Shainie starts tugging at my shirt. Maybe she wants me to play with her.

"Let me find you a good place before it gets too crowded." I'm a bit of an expert now on the best spots — as far as possible from the doors that lead to the broken toilets and as close as possible to the wall.

Once they're settled, I explain how everything works. "There's one free meal a day. Bread and soup, but the soup is more like swill. If you brought food and money, save the food for the journey and spend the money. You can buy cheese when the sellers come. They only let us out a few at a time, so you have to be fast. There's no time to pick and choose. Or bargain. The prices are really high, but if you don't buy something, someone else will."

Elias isn't really listening, but Cecilia is. I can tell she's going to be the one in charge.

"The toilets are pretty awful. The ones inside are broken and the ones outside aren't much better. If the guard is nice, he'll let you go in the field, but watch where you walk, if you know what I mean."

"At least I'm still with my family," Elias mutters. Then he realizes what he just said. He looks so upset that I feel sorry for him. "Oh, Natt, forgive me."

I shrug. "It's okay. I'm glad someone gets to stay with their family. We'll meet up with Papa eventually."

I'm thinking of the fortune teller's words: *You will all be reunited at the end of the war.*

Oh, no! I forgot to check on her. There was so much commotion this morning, with people leaving and the sound of warplanes overhead and the news about Hitler, that I didn't have a chance to think about her.

Now it's too late. She's gone, and I'll never know if she really did die during the night.

Elias sighs. "Well, here we are. Displaced, deported, dismissed. Why the Russians are bothering with us when they need their soldiers and resources to fight the Nazis, I will never understand. Or rather, I do understand. It's the logic of dictators. In other words, no logic."

Cecilia, who's been arranging their things — they have even more than us, if that's possible — stops what she's doing and says in a terrified whisper, "Hush, hush, Elias. How many times do I have to beg you? You have a daughter to think of, if you won't think of me."

"Sorry," he says, but I can tell he's not sorry at all.

"I hope we end up on the same train," I say. "The trains are going to all different parts of Siberia."

Shainie is still tugging at my shirt, and we finally find out why.

"Pee-pee," she says.

Cecilia smiles. "She heard you telling us where the toilets are. What a clever girl!" She kisses Shainie's bouncy black curls. "Natt will take you, won't you, Natt? You're a dear."

I take Shainie's hand, but the door to outside is blocked by the newcomers. Everyone has to be checked off, one by one. There's no way we'll be able to get out anytime soon.

And it's pretty clear from Shainie's squirming that she can't wait much longer.

I turn to the double doors that open onto the corridor. Oh Lord! Not only is there a smell that could strike you dead, but the floor is wet because the toilets have flooded.

"Stinky," Shainie says.

I pick her up and carry her as quickly as I can to a door at the end of the corridor. No matter where it leads, it has to be better than here.

As I get closer, I see that there's a handwritten sign on the door that says NO ENTRY. But the sign is in Russian. And let's say Russian is not a language I know. In that case, I wouldn't be able to read that sign, would I?

I'm just praying the door won't be locked.

And it isn't! In fact, it's one of those swing doors that doesn't have a lock and it leads to a flight of stairs. I run up the stairs with Shainie in my arms.

"Horsie!" she giggles, clinging to my neck.

And all at once we're in a whole other world.

It's paradise up here — so quiet and peaceful. So

private. I'd forgotten how wonderful it is to have privacy, even for a few seconds.

I step into the nearest classroom.

I never knew classrooms could be so beautiful. Rows of polished desks gleam in the dim indoor light, and there's even a piano in the corner. The globe on the teacher's desk reminds me of my old globe, back when I had a room of my own.

Everything in the room is tidy and clean here. It's the exact opposite of downstairs. The opposite of war.

"Pee-pee!" Shainie says.

My eyes land on a bowl of chalk and blackboard erasers on the teacher's desk. I empty it out and place it on the floor.

"You can go in this," I say. "I'll wait outside."

"No. Stay. Stay here," Shainie orders.

When she's finished, she reaches up for me to lift her. Unfortunately, the bowl stays stuck to her bottom for a few seconds, and when it drops back to the floor, it topples over and spills.

Shainie starts laughing. "River!" she squeals. I sweep her away just in time.

I'm so happy to be in this part of the school that I don't want to leave.

"Let's explore," I say, taking her hand. We enter another classroom and I start drawing funny pictures on the blackboard. Mixed-up things, like half-car, half-giraffe. Half-tree, half-mouse. Half-boy, half-bird.

Shainie laughs and claps her hands. "More!" she chirps, every time I finish a drawing.

My eyes keep wandering to a shelf filled with books. I'd borrow one of them if we didn't already have too much luggage. Maybe I could borrow a few just to look at while we're here.

Suddenly I notice a copy of *The Three Musketeers*. It's a shock to see it here. It feels like a hundred years since we acted out scenes from that book, me and Max. How can fighting be so much fun when it's in a book and so horrible in real life?

I want to stay up here, but Shainie makes the mistake of running to the window, and before I can stop her she's climbed on a chair so she can look out. A guard notices her and shouts at us to come down immediately.

Well, it was nice while it lasted. I can sneak up here again when I have to pee. So what if they have to clean up after us when we're gone? They're going to have to clean the whole place anyhow. If they don't want us to make a mess, they should send someone to fix the toilets.

4

Explosion

It's our fifth night here. We're all asleep, or at least trying to sleep, when a terrifying boom rips through the gym.

I don't have to be told what that sound is. Don't ask me how I know. I just do.

Nazi planes are dropping bombs on us.

What happens when a bomb falls on you? Do you die slowly or is it fast? Do you burn to death or do you get squished, or what?

Mama pulls me down to her lap and places a pillow over my head.

"This pillow will keep you safe!" She has to shout because babies are shrieking and little kids are crying.

I know a pillow can't protect me, but I tell myself that it can, and at least it shuts out some of the noise. When I peek out from under the pillow I see everyone crouching over their kids and trying to cover their own heads with luggage or coats.

Eventually the gym calms down. Mama lifts the pillow. "Didn't I tell you we were lucky to be heading east? We'll be so much safer in Siberia, Natty dear."

Bombs are falling from the sky and she's still hoping to fool me into thinking that we're the luckiest people on the planet. And I have to go on pretending that it's working, so she won't be sad about me being sad.

I don't know how much longer either of us can keep it up.

5

Train Two, Carriage One

This morning they herded us onto trucks and drove us to the railway station.

After eleven days at the gym, I think everyone was relieved to be moving at last. It had rained all night, and when I breathed in the heavenly morning air, I felt I was floating.

The Czernowitz train station looks like a white castle, with spires and turrets and hundreds of windows and a big dome in the middle. I used to love coming here. It meant I was on my way to see my grandparents. If only I could be with them now, safe in the mountains, playing badminton!

We've been let out at the large plaza between the station and the track, where two long trains stand waiting for us.

It's crowded here, too, but at least we're outdoors. Friends and relatives of the deportees have come to say goodbye and deliver gifts — mostly food and blankets for the trip.

With all the confusion, you wouldn't think there was any sort of plan in place, but there is. One train is going northeast and the other is going southeast and there's a list of names for each train and each carriage. The guards call out the names on a megaphone, followed by the number of the train (Train One or Train Two) and the number of the carriage the person is supposed to board. We've registered Irena as our cousin, so there's a good chance she'll stay with us.

That's what I'm praying for. Please, please, please let Irena stay with us.

I'm also hoping Shainie and Elias and Cecilia will be with us. Shainie's been following me like a shadow ever since I took her up to the classrooms. I sneaked back there a few times when everyone was buying food, and I borrowed some books to read to her.

Last night I read to her until she fell asleep, and first thing this morning she ran over to our corner and woke me up. Poked me in the shoulder and said, "Natty. Book, please." So it's a good thing we've all ended up together at the railway station, seeing as Shainie's decided she can't live without me. She's been holding on to my sleeve since we put down our luggage.

Even though I know their names will be called eventually, it's a shock when the guard blares out, "Elias Weiss. Cecilia Weiss. Shainie Weiss. Train One, Carriage Five."

I'm relieved that Elias and Cecilia are together. Some of the women are being separated from their husbands, and there's a lot of weeping and wailing. "There must be a mistake," they plead. "That's my husband. Please let me go with him. I'll be useful, I'll work hard, I promise. I'm strong."

But the guards ignore them, or else tell them to be quiet.

Cecilia tries to lift Shainie, but Shainie refuses to let go of my sleeve. Cecilia sighs and turns to us. "Maybe you'll also be in Train One, and then maybe we can switch carriages. Let's wait until your names are called." There's so much going on that no one notices if you don't board right away.

In fact, it wouldn't be hard to escape now. We could easily run away. But where would we go? If they catch us, they'll send us to the Gulag. Irena says there are at least fifty gulag prisons, maybe even a hundred, so we probably wouldn't even be sent to the one Papa's at.

Besides, if the Nazis are invading, it's no longer safe here for anyone, especially Jews.

"Read the book," Shainie says, as if nothing special is going on.

I haven't been able to bring any of the books, and I wouldn't be able to read to her anyhow. It's too crowded and noisy, and we have to keep our eyes on our luggage.

"I'll tell you a story," I say. "Once upon a time there was an old woman who lived in a castle. One day when she was —"

Before I can finish the sentence, we hear our names. "Sophia Silver. Nathan Silver. Irena Drabik. Train Two, Carriage One."

My stomach does a double somersault, and for a minute I think I'm going to be sick. Shainie's going on a different train, to a different part of Siberia, and there's nothing I can do about it. If the wives and husbands can't manage to switch trains, no one can.

It's my fault. Instead of praying for Irena to stay with us, I should have prayed not to be separated from Shainie.

Not that God — if there is a God — is listening to anyone's prayers right now.

Cecilia bends down. There are tears running down her cheeks, but she wipes them away quickly.

"Listen, *mama'le*," she says. "You have to kiss Natt goodbye now. We'll see him again after our trip."

"I'm not saying goodbye," Shainie says. "I'm staying with Natty."

Cecilia looks at us helplessly.

I whisper in Shainie's ear, "If you go like a good girl, I'll read you twenty books."

I'm making her think it's going to be soon. I'm basically lying to her.

It sort of works. She nods her head and lets go of

my sleeve. But I can tell she doesn't want to leave.

I feel a million times worse than when I turned away from Papa. As soon as Shainie's train starts moving, she'll know that I lied to her, and she'll scream and call out for me, and I won't be there.

Swallowing tears, I follow my mother to Train Two, Carriage One.

There's a ramp at the entrance of each carriage. The entrance is right in the middle of the carriage.

"It's a train for livestock," some people behind me are grumbling.

The train looked really high when we were on the platform, but once we've dragged our luggage up the ramp, I see that the ceiling is actually quite low.

"Oh, how lucky," Mama says. "Look, darling — beds. They've built us bunk beds. We can sleep the entire way."

Beds? I'm not sure anyone else would call these contraptions beds. *Shelf* might be more accurate.

There are three bunks in each frame, and the part we're supposed to lie on is just two or three wooden beams with big spaces between them.

In fact, the entire carriage is made of wood. The walls, the ceiling, the floor. Dark, dirty wood.

There's not even enough space to sit up on the bottom two bunks. You'd feel you were in a coffin, lying on them. Or maybe I'm thinking of coffins because of how narrow they are.

We're among the first ones inside, but I can tell it's going to be ridiculously crammed. There are two rows of these bunks on either side of the carriage, six in each row, perpendicular to the wall. They're only two or three inches apart.

That's thirty-six people in one carriage. More, if you count babies and little kids, who don't get a bed of their own. The aisle between the rows is so narrow you practically have to walk sideways.

The only windows are four little rectangles, way up high. They don't have any glass in them. They're just holes.

I think of the train that took me to the Carpathian Mountains to see my grandparents. I'd watch the landscape chug by as if it wasn't us moving, but the trees and fields and grazing cows.

I thought we would be on the same type of train to Siberia. But this train is the exact opposite of the train to Viznitsa. It's like expecting to go to a vacation resort by the sea and being thrown into a dungeon instead.

The people behind me were right. This is a train for animals. There's even straw on the floor.

It's getting harder to hold back tears. But Mama is going on and on about the bedding.

"What luck that we brought all those quilts and pillows. They'll really come in handy now," she's saying. "We'll make it nice and comfy."

Irena has meanwhile chosen a bunk near one of

the window openings, on the side facing the station.

"Climb up here, Natt," she says. "Children need fresh air, and it's easiest for you to get up and down."

We spread our blankets and quilts and coats on the boards. We need to keep our coats with us at all times, because that's where our money is hidden, in the seams. Mama also keeps money inside her shirt for whatever we need now. That way she doesn't have to keep ripping open the seams and then sewing them back with people around.

For once, Mama's right. We're never going to be comfy, but it's a good thing we brought all these bedclothes. The pillows and quilts made a big difference in the gym and they make even more of a difference here. The bunks look a little less scary now. They're still very narrow, but maybe I won't feel the spaces between the beams.

Poor Irena — she didn't bring much. She only has one quilt, but she insists she's fine. We give her a sheet and she's made a pillow out of her coat.

I settle myself on my new bed. It's boiling hot and the entire carriage reeks of farm animals. Not that nice smell you get in barns. More of a diarrhea smell.

At least I'm near a window. There's not much air coming in at the moment, but I can look out at the platform and see what's going on. The deportees have all boarded by now, and the friends and relatives are being told to clear out.

A guard comes on board and asks for two people who speak Russian to be our representatives. Irena immediately volunteers. Her Russian isn't as good as mine, but even over the past three days she's improved a lot. She's a fast learner.

I can tell that the guard had someone older in mind. He's about to object, but a few people start saying, "*Da, tak*, Irena," so he shrugs and writes down her name. I'm proud that she's with us.

"Anyone else?" he snaps.

An old man comes forward. His Russian is perfect, but his hands shake and he walks with a cane.

"I'm a geologist," he says.

The guard shrugs again and writes the geologist's name next to Irena's. "You are to report to us on the health of the passengers and on any special situations. You'll be in charge of food and water distribution and general communication."

He jumps off the train and bolts the door. We're locked in now.

"He has to lock the doors so they don't slide open while we're moving," Mama explains. She's standing next to the bunk and she takes my hand in hers, but I don't mind. Even if she sang me a lullaby I probably wouldn't care. I'd shut my eyes and pretend I was a tiny kid again.

6

Don't Smile, Lenin

I'm curled up on my bunk dreaming about Aunt Dora's apple strudel when a sledgehammer smashes into my head. Or that's what it feels like.

In fact, it's a loud noise. And the noise is the most blood-curdling, heart-stopping sound I have ever heard. It's a hundred times worse than when we were in the gym, because it feels a hundred times closer. It feels as if bombs are going to land right on the train.

"Everyone stay calm," Irena says in her teacher voice. "Explosions are always much farther away than they seem. Sound carries."

I want to believe her, so I do. But when I climb up to the window hole and squint out, I see that she's wrong.

The Nazis are attacking the train station.

Russian soldiers are running every which way, as if they can't decide what to do or where to go. There's a lot of shouting and pointing to the sky. They're setting up machine guns at either end of the plaza, though how that's going to help, I'm not sure.

And then there's a different noise — an awful kind of whining that makes your eyes hurt.

The soldiers dive down and hide under the train. A few seconds later, I hear a rattle that reminds me of the dried peas in Papa's warehouse when they poured down the chute.

Machine guns are spraying the station from the sky, while other planes are dropping what look like metal loaves of bread. The loaves explode with a burst of fire when they hit the ground. There are more flashes of fire and billows of smoke, and I see soldiers lying or sitting on the ground, screaming.

Irena and my mother pull me away from the window, and the three of us crouch together on the bottom bunk. The cries of wounded people make me feel seasick. I pray for it to stop.

Mama covers my head again with her magic pillow. She says calmly, "Now you're safe, darling. This pillow won't let anything happen to you."

It's not logical, I know it isn't, but right at this minute I'm ready to believe in magic pillows.

Finally, the roar of weapons is replaced by a long, steady siren, and I hear calls of "all-clear." I've never heard that phrase before, but I know I'm going to love it for the rest of my life.

It was a truly dirty trick, the pact between Hitler and Stalin. Hitler just wanted to invade Poland without having to worry that the Russians would try to stop him. Or prepare for being invaded themselves. And it worked. Russia is so unprepared that Russian soldiers have to hide under a train.

Hitler wants to conquer not just Europe but also Russia and Asia — and then the whole entire world.

When I open my eyes and lift my head from under the pillow, Clop-Clop is lying next to me.

That was the surprise Mama was saving for me. My poor, dear Mama! She really thinks my old toy horse can make me happy now.

Yes, I loved that horse when I was little. I slept with him, ate with him, and when I went off to kindergarten I kissed him goodbye and promised I'd be back soon.

But I was five years old.

In a way it's nice to see him here, but at the same time he makes me feel lonelier than ever. Of course, I have to act as if I'm wild with joy for Mama's sake.

As I hold Clop-Clop to my chest, I start thinking about Papa. He must have been on a train just like this one. Did the Germans attack that train, too? If only we could write him a letter! He won't even know where we are, and we don't really know where he is.

And to think that I missed my only chance to show him how much I love him ...

And all because of that Pioneer business, which turned out to be a big stupid nothing. What an idiot I was! If anything happens to him, and that's the last thing he remembers about me, I'll just lie down and die.

I return to my post by the window hole. It's getting hotter by the second and I'm dripping with sweat. I remove my shoes and tear off my shirt and my socks.

I hear some of the deportees calling for help farther down the train. But the soldiers ignore them. Instead they begin clearing away the mess on the platform and taking care of each other. They signal with their arms and shout instructions for the train to leave.

I hope Shainie and her parents are all right. Poor Shainie. At least she doesn't understand what's going on. Maybe Cecilia put a magic pillow over her head, too.

I glance around at the other deportees in our carriage. I'm hoping for a kid my own age. But there's only a toddler with his grandparents.

Baby Anna Fischer is here, too.

Mostly we've got old women and a few old men.

In the far corner there's a priest from our town. Papa often used to stop and chat with him. He has a square white beard and he's still wearing his long gray robe, even though his church was converted into a government office. The big cross that used to hang around his neck is missing, or maybe it's tucked in-side his robe.

I also recognize the town pharmacist, and Andreas the Tall, who used to visit our tenant Mr. Jacobson long ago. Those stories we used to invent, me and Max, about Andreas the Tall and Bruno the Bald, splitting our sides at some of them. It's as if it all happened in another life, a life that I only read about in some book long ago. I'm starting to forget who I am, because now that my old life is gone, I'm not sure what's left. I'm slowly drifting away from myself.

Andreas is on a top bunk like me. He's reading *The Magic Mountain* — I recognize the cover from our bookshelves at home, when we had a home. I call out to him and he looks up from the book. He seems glad to see me, and he comes over to talk to Mama. He has to crouch a little, because he's too tall for the carriage.

The nearly toothless old woman right next to me, who's on her own, and who from her ragged, dirty clothes seems to be a poor Ukrainian peasant, has brought an actual mattress with her.

How did she carry it? Maybe on her head. It doesn't look like she had much else to bring. The mattress is too long and wide for the boards, so she's folded in the edges. She's lying on her back on the lumpy mattress with a peaceful expression on her face. I can imagine Max's brother Michael drawing her the way she looks now, smiling on her strange bed. Mattress Woman in Train Two.

I open my schoolbag and see that my aunt accidentally stuffed Max's going-away presents back into his bag instead of into mine. I can tell by the half-torn picture of Lenin on the inside flap. I study Lenin's smiling face and try to decide whether I'm angry with him or not.

Comrade Minsky said Lenin saw himself as a lantern. Poor people were in the dark about how it isn't fair to slave away so that the rich can get richer. Lenin wanted to enlighten the starving peasants so they'd do something about all the injustice.

Comrade Minsky never said anything about Stalin. Thinking back, I realize that he was afraid of getting into trouble. Maybe he was already in trouble, and that's why he had to leave his family and his university job.

Maybe the thing he was afraid to say was that Stalin is the opposite of Lenin. Lenin wanted to bring light. Stalin wants to plunge everything into darkness.

"Don't smile, Lenin," I say out loud, looking at his cheery face, or what's left of it. "There's nothing to smile about. Your revolution is a mess."

I must be losing my mind, talking to a picture.

Inside the bag, I find the chocolate wafers. I forgot I had those.

"Thank you, Max," I say. If I can talk to Lenin, I can talk to Max. I hope he and his family are on their way to Switzerland by now. Maybe their papers finally came through.

I bite into a wafer and eat as slowly as I can to make it last. I offer the package to Irena and Mama. Irena accepts just one, but Mama refuses.

"Enjoy every bite," she says.

There's another treasure in the schoolbag. It's something I didn't even think I'd need, but it turns out to be a lifesaver, like Mrs. Shapira's handkerchief in the cell. It's the Camphor Balm for Man or Beast. It has a really powerful smell, and if I hold it to my nose, I get a break from the sickening smell in the carriage.

At last, with a very loud clang, the train begins to chug forward. And with every chug we move farther away from all the places that I know and love.

Other people are also eating. The smell of sausage drifts over from the Mattress Woman. I wonder how she can be a Class Enemy. I'm sure she's never had a penny to her name.

She leans across and offers me a slice. The sausage looks like you'd grow a tail if you ate it, and I don't think she's washed her hands in the past decade, but I'm so hungry I almost take it. We're not really supposed to eat pork, but that's not why I say no. Mama told me not to take food and not to offer it.

She said that because of the war, the rules of sharing have changed.

"Thank you, I'm not hungry," I lie.

Even though we're moving, it's at such a slow pace that someone could easily walk alongside the train and keep up with us. It keeps getting hotter, too, and the window openings don't help at all.

I need to use the toilet but have no idea where it is.

"Mama," I whisper.

She's asleep and doesn't hear me, but Irena does.

"What is it?" she asks.

"Where's the toilet?"

Irena slides out from the middle bunk and stands up. "It's not the greatest arrangement, I'm afraid, but it's all there is. It's the barrel next to the luggage."

Right in the middle of the train floor are two round, knee-high wooden containers.

"No, those are for water," I tell her.

"The barrel near the doors is water," Irena says. "The other one is — well, it's our toilet. We'll empty it as soon as the train stops."

I stare at the barrels in horror. This can't be right.

"But everyone can see!" I protest.

"If we had a saw, we could make a hole in the floor. I'll ask for one when we reach a station. But for now, this is all we have. I'll hold a sheet up if you like," she offers.

I don't know what's worse. Going in public, or having Irena hold up a sheet, which in any case will only protect me from one side.

While I'm deciding, the old priest walks over to the barrel and lifts his robe. I turn away. I feel hot and cold at the same time, and blood rushes to my head. A priest is going in a barrel! In front of everyone!

It's as if we're animals. That's what it's come to, and that's why they've put us on an animal train. Our feelings don't come into it. Disgusting food, dirty water, a miserable place to relieve oursleves. That's all we get, and if we die, no one cares. Because we're not humans anymore. We're deportees. Deportees are one step below human.

I should have figured it out sooner, the moment I found out about the quota. A quota isn't about people. It's about numbers. That's what we are: numbers. That's probably why that poor peasant is here. Not because she's an Enemy of the State or related to one. She's here because Stalin set a quota.

"Tell me when the priest is finished," I whisper. I'm thinking it must be worse for him. I'm just a kid. He's an adult and a church person everyone is supposed to look up to.

"He's done," Irena tells me.

I walk over to the barrel, trying to persuade myself that no one will look at me. They will all turn away, as I did.

But when I come closer and see how wide the barrel is, I get terrified that I'll fall inside.

"I need to hold on to something," I tell Irena. "I might fall in."

"I've got an idea." She calls out, "Does anyone have a rope or something we can use as a rope?"

"I have a cloth belt," someone replies faintly. It's Baby Anna's mother. She's thin and pale and she's wound a long red scarf around her head.

Irena accepts the belt and ties it to the bed frame closest to the barrel. I feel sorry for the people who have bunks on either side of the barrel. One of them is occupied by the toddler and his grandparents. They all seem to be asleep. Small mercies, as my mother would say.

Irena makes a special kind of knot.

"This is our safety rope," she tells everyone. "You can hold onto it for balance. Thank you, Mrs. ...?"

"Felicia," the mother says. She's rocking Baby Anna in her arms. I'm glad Baby Anna doesn't know anything, not even that it smells bad here.

"Thank you, Felicia. This is a great help."

Amazing, but none of this craziness has woken Mama, who's out like a log. I don't think she slept much at the gym. In the end, I'm glad it's Irena helping me. Mama would have tried to convince me that the barrel was a wonderful idea and weren't we lucky that we didn't have to relieve ourselves on the floor.

But after all that, I can't go. The whole thing is just too awful.

I climb back up to my bed, stepping carefully on the edge of the frame and hoping it doesn't collapse. I'm happy for Mama that she's asleep. I get the feeling sleep is going to be the only bearable part of this trip.

If Mama's right about microbes, how will we survive? The water in the drinking barrel can't possibly be clean. Mama and I have our own cup, but most people are using a tin cup that's hanging on a nail. Not only are they all using the same cup, but the cup itself is rusty and dirty, and on top of that, no one can wash their hands, even after using the toilet barrel, and everyone's hands touch the water when they dip the cup in.

Well, maybe it doesn't matter. If what we feel and think no longer matters, maybe it also doesn't matter if we all get typhoid and dysentery.

Irena says, "Can I climb up and join you? It's very cramped down here." That's when I realize that I'm hugging myself and rocking. I didn't even notice I was doing it.

Irena comes up and sits cross-legged next to me. She suggests we read *War and Peace* together so she can improve her Russian, but I can't concentrate. I'm too hot and too miserable.

"How about we do some schoolwork?" she coaxes. "Nature studies, for example. We can look out the window and I'll teach you about the things we see."

We're mostly passing boring farmland and fields, with forests and gray mountains behind them. But Irena knows a lot about different types of clouds and trees and what grows where. I like her voice, and I like learning.

I wonder if there will be schools in Siberia. I thought there would be, but now I'm not sure. I'm not sure about anything anymore.

7

Our First Stop

The priest is dead. He died during the night, but we can't report his death because the train is still moving.

What if his body starts to rot, like that dead polecat Max and I once came across?

Especially since it's like an oven in here. We might *all* die, in fact, just from the heat.

Irena is the one who noticed that the priest was gone. She was checking up on everyone this morning and when she got to him, she saw that he'd passed away in the night. Some people began to pray and chant and cry. The Mattress Woman swayed from side to side, muttering to herself.

At least he was old. At least he won't have to use the barrel anymore.

And he won't have to go to Siberia, where the temperature is probably minus a thousand. Though at this point, I can't imagine being too cold. All I long for, twenty-four hours a day, is cold.

The heat is worse than the hunger. We've all pretty much finished the food we brought. It's sad, but also irritating, to hear the little kid, Ivan, constantly complaining, *ya holodni, ya holodni*. I'm hungry, I'm hungry. It's getting on everyone's nerves.

"Does anyone mind if I go through the Reverend Father's things?" Irena's cheerful, matter-of-fact voice rings out like a bell.

No one says anything, so she rummages inside his bag. All she finds is clothes, a toothbrush and some cheese.

"Does anyone object if this cheese goes to the nursing mother and the child?" Irena continues. She means Ivan.

No one answers that question either, though I'm sure everyone wants little Ivan to quit whining, if nothing else. I'm so hungry I could eat a tree, but I don't want cheese from a dead man's bag.

Irena hands one half of the cheese to Felicia, who tries to smile but doesn't really succeed, and the other half to Ivan, who really does smile. He grabs the cheese with his tiny hands, and I think it cheers us all up to see him biting into it and saying, "Yum yum."

Max used to say that all the time when he ate, but in a funny way. He'd cross his eyes and go *yummy, yummy,* or else he'd rub his belly and say, *my stomach's in love.*

I decide to write him a letter. I hope he never gets it, because with luck he's in Switzerland by now. But I feel like writing to him anyhow. Maybe when we reach a station one of the guards will agree to post it for me.

I sharpen a pencil and begin: *Hello there, Max!*

Then I stop. I stare down at the blank page and the blank page stares back.

What do I say? I can't tell him how bad things are, because we could get into trouble, and besides, it would upset him. But what's the point of writing if I don't tell him the truth? I'm ready to hide the truth from Mama, but not from Max.

I also don't have a return address, other than *Train Two, Carriage One, Hell.* It occurs to me that I have no idea what country I live in anymore. Maybe no country.

I'd like to write to Lucy, too, but Andreas the Tall told me that she's gone to stay with her uncle, the one who owns the cosmetics factory in Budapest. I wish I'd asked her for the name of that factory.

Suddenly, everyone goes silent. The train has been moving so slowly that at first I'm not sure if it's really come to a complete stop. But it has.

"We're at a station!" Irena is so excited, her voice climbs at least an octave as she announces the news.

I peer out of the window hole. It's true! We've reached a small station surrounded by fields.

Ivan's grandmother, who hasn't uttered a word until now, stands up, raises her arms above her head and cries out, "God is merciful!"

Seconds later we hear the door latch scrape and slide, and the two big doors in the middle of the carriage fly open.

Air!

We run to the entrance and lean out. Even though it's a small station, the platform is crowded with farmers who are there to sell food. I can smell the cheese and boiled potatoes and pickled cabbage from up here.

A guard sets up a ramp and climbs into our carriage. Irena smiles sweetly and tells him about the priest. The guard doesn't smile back, but I can tell by his eyes that he likes her.

The guard summons two soldiers and they take the priest out on a stretcher. I notice a whole pile of stretchers on the platform, lying one on top of the other.

Do they expect masses of people to die on the trains?

I guess everyone's thinking the same thing, because Irena says in a loud, stern voice, as though we're children who have been misbehaving, "Stretchers are always needed in wartime."

We begin calling to the farmers, who move up and down the platform with their baskets and wheelbarrows. The prices are three times what we had to pay at the gym. Everyone grumbles, but we have no choice. We have to pay what they ask. Twenty-five rubles for a large potato, thirty for a quart of milk.

Mama buys three loaves of bread, lots of cheese, a few boiled potatoes and some pickled chives. She hands me a piece of bread and two chives.

"Eat slowly," she warns me, "or you'll get a terrible stomach ache." She wraps the rest of the food in a sweater and stuffs it into our knapsack.

The chives are surprisingly delicious. So is the bread.

"They have to charge a lot," my mother says. "They're poor themselves, and it's harder to grow food out here."

Andreas and the toddler's grandfather remove the disgusting toilet barrel together. I'm praying they don't accidentally drop it.

Irena speaks in a low voice to the guard. He nods and disappears. A few minutes later he jumps on board with some tools and chisels a small hole in the floor.

Now our toilet is a hole in the floor, covered by a board so we don't fall down onto the tracks. We'll still be exposed — maybe even more than before — but at least we can leave our "bodily secretions," as Mama calls them, behind. The toilet barrel is gone for good.

Irena whispers to the guard, and he allows her to get off the train. The ramp is gone now, so he holds her by the waist and swings her down. Then he points out a stout man who is a little better dressed than the farmers, and Irena goes up to him. The two of them walk to the end of the platform, away from the crowd, and I see her pull something out of her shirt.

It's the priest's cross! The one he wore around his neck. It was there after all, tucked inside his robe.

Everyone else is too busy to notice. I watch Irena and the man out of the corner of my eye while I help pass food and money between the farmers who are reaching up and the passengers who are reaching down.

I can tell the well-dressed man is interested in the cross. He hands over some paper notes and coins. Irena stuffs some of them in her shirt. With the rest she buys bread, cheese, boiled potatoes, a big jar of milk and, after some haggling, a cup. When she returns, I reach down and carefully take the jar from her.

Irena divides the food into two parts. She gives one part to Felicia and one part to Ivan's grandparents. The gratitude in Felicia's eyes is almost embarrassing. Then she pours milk for me and Felicia and Ivan. I gulp down two cups almost in one go.

Milk has never tasted this good. As a bonus, the cup is clean, more or less.

It's amazing how fast the food gets sold. Everyone cooperates and everyone's honest. We all get the right change and exactly what we ask for. People keep grumbling about the prices, but we're glad to have food.

When the selling's done, a soldier brings a huge pot of soup and tin bowls. The soup is for all of us, though the people who couldn't afford to buy anything, like the Mattress Woman, are the ones who need it the most.

The soldier ladles the soup into bowls. I can tell by his expression that he hates his job, hates the army, hates us, hates everything that's happening. But when Ivan points to him and says, "Papa," he forgets to be angry for a second or two, and he almost smiles.

"His father is a soldier in the Russian army," Ivan's grandfather explains.

So even the families of soldiers are getting deported! Or maybe it's a mistake. Maybe someone wrote down the wrong name.

Mistake or not, it's obvious by now that once you're on a list, you stay there. Stalin doesn't care if your life is ruined by a slip of the pen.

The soup Irena hands out looks so vile, with slimy bits of old cabbage and dirty carrot, that I offer my bowl to the Mattress Woman. She gladly takes the extra portion.

We also get a chunk of bread each.

"They'd give us more," Mama says, "but they can't afford it. All the food is going to feed the army."

Then the doors close, and we're trapped once again in the infernal heat.

I lie down, shut my eyes and fall into a strange dream. Comrade Minsky is standing in the snow, teaching us arithmetic. I worry that he's going to catch pneumonia, but it turns out that it's a type of hot snow that Marx invented to keep the masses warm. Then Comrade Martha shows up dragging a mattress behind her. There's a dog on the mattress who looks just like Zoomie, but he's smaller and skinnier, as if no one is feeding him. Comrade Martha says, *Now we're going to see a movie the Party made just for us.*

And there on the screen are all the things I used to have. All my games and nature treasures, and my house and everything in the house, like the radio and the dishes and even the dusters, and then Zoomie and the warehouse and Lana and my desk at school and Lucy and Max …

Lucy and Max are waving at me in the movie, and Comrade Minsky is mumbling, *Minus a thousand, minus a thousand*, and I don't know if he means the thousand things I've lost or the temperature in Siberia.

Or a thousand bugs. Because suddenly there are tiny brown bugs crawling on my body.

Not in my dream. In real life.

I jump up and shriek.

I'm not the only one. All around me people are roaring and swearing. The worst swear words imaginable, in every language they know.

We're being attacked by bugs. Dark creatures the size of sesame seeds are crawling all over the walls, all over our things and all over us.

Where did they come from? How did they appear out of nowhere?

Everyone, including Mama, is frantically trying to whisk them off and stomp on them. Mama isn't screaming, but her eyes are wider than I've ever seen them.

Only Irena is calm. "It seems we have an infestation of body lice," she announces loudly. "Please try not to panic. You're frightening the children."

"It's her. *She* brought them in her mattress," a muscular old man shouts in Romanian. He points to my neighbor and shakes a fist at her.

Luckily, the Mattress Woman doesn't understand Romanian, or else she's deaf. Or maybe she's used to having people shake their fists at her.

"They don't live in mattresses," Irena says in Romanian and then in Ukrainian. "They're not bed bugs. They were obviously here from the previous passengers."

The old man grunts spitefully, "Why should I trust you? What do you Jews know?"

Heads turn when he says that. More than half of us are Jews — though not, as it happens, Irena.

Irena smiles politely. "I'm as Christian as you," she tells him, "if that's any consolation, though why it should be, I can't say. Jews know as much and as little as anyone else. Please, let's all try to get along. Arguing among ourselves is only going to make us hotter."

I realize I have to accept the lice. We all do.

We have no choice, because we can't get rid of them. All we can do is try to kill as many as possible. Mama says if you kill one, you're killing all its descendants, too, so it's really like killing a million each time you squish one.

Life with bugs. A new thing for me — though not, as far as I can tell, for my neighbor. She's the only one who doesn't seem to notice the bugs. She doesn't even seem to be itchy, whereas I'm so itchy I want to slap myself into a coma.

Poor Max! I remember his imaginary bugs. Maybe he had some kind of sixth sense about the future — or my future, anyhow.

Even though the doors are closed now, the train isn't moving. We're all wondering why we're stuck here, sweltering in the heat.

At last a soldier opens the doors and tells us, "We won't be setting off until nightfall, so I'm leaving the doors open. Anyone who tries to escape will be arrested. Hitler's on the move. Get ready for raids."

"Hitler good, good," the Mattress Woman mumbles, tearing at her bread and sucking on it.

Luckily no one's heard her, apart from me. How can she be on Hitler's side? Doesn't she know who he is and what he stands for, and that he's the one attacking us?

I guess she doesn't know much about anything. She probably thinks the moon is made of cheese and Stalin is a movie star.

At least the doors are open now. Some of us stand or sit at the opening, breathing in the evening air. The sellers have left, and it's only soldiers on the platform now, running around and looking nervous. There isn't much of a town here. All I can see are a few farmhouses in the distance.

When the soldier who brought our soup passes by, I raise my hand.

"Yes?" he says.

"Please may I go to the toilet over there?" I point to a little cluster of trees behind the station.

He shrugs. "All right, but if a bullet hits you, don't blame me." He lifts me off the train with his strong hands and I run over to the trees.

It's so wonderful to touch a tree and feel the leaves on my face. It's cooler here, too, than on the train. And no bugs.

If only they'd let us stay in this village for the rest of the war!

I dig a bit of a hole in the ground with my shoe, crouch down … and finally I can go.

At least that's done. It's not perfect — no paper, and I can't wash my hands — but it's a million times better than the carriage.

I'd love to breathe the country air for a few more minutes, but what if the train leaves without me? So I hurry back, climb up to my moldy, filthy, bug-infested bunk and look out the window. Irena joins me with a bundle and a pair of scissors and brings a finger to her lips.

The bundle turns out to be the priest's spare cassock, his pajamas and a pair of long johns.

"Felicia desperately needs more diapers," Irena whispers. "There's no way to wash the ones she brought with her. I'm convinced the Reverend Father wouldn't mind. It's what Jesus would want, too, if he were here."

So we sit there and quietly cut and rip the clothing into nappy-sized squares.

I hope Irena's right. I hope if the priest can see us from the other side, he won't mind that we're using his cassock for Baby Anna.

Even if he can't see us, even if there is no other side, I still hope he wouldn't mind.

8

Fights

Three weeks. We've been on this train for three weeks.

And this is the third argument in less than an hour.

Disagreements break out a lot now, even though there aren't as many of us. After the priest, seven more passengers in our carriage, all of them old, died in their sleep, including the geologist who represented us, and Andreas's mother. I didn't even know his mother was with him. He cried the entire day. Then he went back to reading *The Magic Mountain*.

Most arguments are about food. The old man who accused the Mattress Woman of bringing lice, and who made the comment about Jews, keeps thinking people are stealing his food. He has to be reminded that he ate the food himself — not that he believes anyone. He says there's a conspiracy and we're all in on it.

More than once, Irena found the cheese he thought someone had stolen under his blankets, but instead of thanking her, he accused her of "sleight of hand." That's one of his favorite expressions.

This morning, Irena finally lost her temper. "You're worse than some of the five-year-olds I've taught!" she yelled, and everyone in the car applauded.

Needless to say, that did not help matters.

Right now Ivan's grandfather and Andreas are the ones fighting. Ivan's grandfather is angry that Andreas bribed a guard to let him eat a hot meal in the canteen at the last station we were at and didn't even think of bringing something back for little Ivan when he knew the grandfather would have gladly paid for it. Doesn't Andreas see how hungry the boy is?

Andreas is saying that none of the food was transportable, and that anyway, he didn't have permission to take it out of the canteen. He says he didn't feel like getting sent to the Gulag for disobedience, and that he needed a hot meal because he's been feeling feverish ever since his mother died.

Insults fly back and forth. I stop listening. Usually Irena manages to sort out arguments, but at the moment she's either sleeping or too fed up to bother. The good thing is that the quarrels never last very long. No one has the energy.

My life is a bit of a blur. I sleep, eat, kill lice and scratch myself half to death. I have big red welts all over my body, and one of my ears is the size of a cauliflower from mosquito bites.

Yes, mosquitoes and flies have joined the wildlife invasion.

To distract myself and pass the time, I study with Irena. She explains molecules and the difference between solids, liquids and gases, and how the Table of Elements works. I had no idea that everything on the entire planet was made up of elements, and that there aren't even that many.

I've discovered that facts are relaxing. They don't change and they don't let you down. Without Irena's lessons, I'd definitely lose what little sanity I've managed to hold on to.

Mama stubbed her toe in the dark and the swelling became infected. It's a good thing we had Max's ointments and bandages.

What else? Oh, yes. It rained a few times, and I got wet, which helped me cool down, but my blankets and pillow got all soggy. Also, I keep getting pins and needles in my arms and legs.

The biggest event in our lives is arriving at a station and buying food. Bit by bit, Irena's been handing out the money she received for the cross, so that everyone can buy something, even the Mattress Woman. The free soup is as disgusting as ever, but sometimes I dip my bread in it. One woman found a fish eye in her bowl. She was not happy.

I spend a lot of time with the sliding puzzle Max gave me, trying to find the fastest way to get the numbers in order. I'm getting pretty good at it.

I miss Max so much. I like to picture him in Switzerland, surrounded by ice-capped mountains. Maybe he'll even learn to ski.

I think a lot these days about what Papa said. In wartime, just getting through the day makes you a hero. But I don't feel like a hero. I think it's the opposite, really. War makes you feel smaller and smaller. You keep shrinking, like Alice in Wonderland, until you're so small you're practically invisible.

A person that tiny can't be a hero.

That's what I'm thinking about as I fall into a strange kind of half-sleep. That happens to me a lot these days. I'm mostly asleep but I can feel the lice in my dreams and I know I'm tossing and turning and trying to shake them off.

In my half-sleep Mama is saying, "How lucky that there was an eye in the soup. That way, we can be sure that someone is watching over us." And as she says it she does a little dance right there next to my bunk.

Suddenly, in my dream, I feel my blood boiling with rage. This is the last straw! I can't take her lies one minute longer. She's wearing a sorcerer's hat on her head, and she holds up a picture of snow on the Alps, hoping to cool me that way.

I begin to shout at her. "We're not lucky! We had a house, we had horses, we had a warehouse with chutes. I had Max and Lucy and a telescope. Now Papa's in the Gulag and I'm hungry and dirty and crawling with bugs and the train smells like a sewer. And no one cares — *no one* — because bombs are dropping from the sky, maybe even on Max and Zoomie and everyone we know. We're not lucky, Mama! Being alive isn't lucky, if this is what life is like."

Mama begins to cry and I reach out to her, but she's a spirit from another world, and my arm goes right through her ...

"Natt! Natt!" I open my eyes. Irena and my mother are both trying to wake me.

Thank heavens it was only a dream. Thank heavens I didn't say all those awful things to my poor mama.

"Guess what, darling? We're going swimming!"

Am I still dreaming? Or is this another one of my mother's inventions?

If it's true, why are her eyes filled with tears?

But Irena laughs and nods. Her words come rushing out so fast that I have to struggle to keep up with her.

"There's-a-lake-at-this-station! They're-letting-everyone-go-into-the-water-to-wash! We-have-five-whole-hours-to-clean-ourselves, clean-our-clothes, can-you-believe-it?"

I sit up. The carriage is nearly empty. I slept right through the commotion.

"Hurry," Mama says. "We don't want to miss a single minute."

9

The Crystal Lake

Outside, a huge crowd is moving toward the lake behind the station. We quickly join them.

The lake is a pure, deep blue, and so clear you can see clouds reflected on the surface. Crystal clouds, floating on water. Beyond the lake there's a pine forest, and in the distance white and green mountains rise up to the sky.

It's like the Schiller poem Max read at my birthday party, a million years ago.

A bridge of pearls rises
Above a misty sea ...

Some boys are calling out to me. It's Julian and Carl and other boys from the gym. Have we really been on the same train this entire time? When you can't communicate with the outside world, you start believing that everyone you've ever known exists in another galaxy.

How different they look — so pale and skinny!

"Natt! Come on!" they shout.

I'm a bit unsteady on my legs at first, and a little scared. I don't know what lies at the bottom of the lake, or how deep it is.

But then, as if someone has whispered in my ear, the words of the fortune teller come back to me: *Be careful but not afraid.* Before long I feel the shockingly cold water around my ankles, then my knees.

Then Julian pulls me down and I'm sitting on the pebbly floor of the lake right up to my neck.

I've never felt so good in my whole, entire life.

The sweat, the dirt, the bugs, the bites — it's all getting washed away. The truth is, I didn't want to admit how filthy and smelly we all were, but now it's safe to think it. No one's been able to wash for weeks.

A little way ahead, Felicia is up to her waist in the water. She looks happy for the first time. At last she's able to wash her baby properly. Baby Anna gurgles as her mother gently splashes water on her.

Several bars of yellow soap appear among the adults, and we pull off our outer clothes and hand them over to be scrubbed.

I'm chatting with my friends. We're comparing notes: disgusting toilets, disgusting food, disgusting rashes, disgusting drinking water. Everyone has a story: vomiting stories, diarrhea stories, bug stories. Even corpse stories. We make fun of the so-called beds and the so-called windows.

It's like a million-pound weight being lifted from my shoulders, talking to the other kids about everything.

All of a sudden, I hear a high-pitched voice squealing, "NATTY! NATTY! NATTY! NATTY!"

I look over my shoulder. Are my eyes and ears playing tricks on me?

"Shainie!" I gasp.

It's really her. No longer as chubby, but with the same bouncy curls and big dark eyes. She starts running to me in the water, and her mother has to hold her back so she won't go in too deep.

I hurry toward them.

"Tell the story, tell the story," Shainie yelps, reaching out to me with both arms.

"I thought you were in Train Two," I say, taking her hand.

Cecilia laughs. "Such luck, Natt! We overheard two guards talking about a brother and sister who ran away. They escaped at the station. So we asked if we could take their place, because they were in Train One. A couple of ten-ruble notes changed hands, and presto! The guards let us switch. Where's your mother?"

"Washing our clothes and things."

"If I'd known that we had this to look forward to … But they don't tell us much, do they?" Cecilia waves to Elias, who's swimming in the distance.

"Tell the story, tell the story," Shainie repeats, tugging at my hand. "Once upon a time there was an old woman in the castle and…?"

Poor Shainie! All this time she's kept that sentence in her head and waited for me to continue.

"In a second, Shainie," I say. I've just had an idea. "Eight people in our carriage are gone," I tell Cecilia. "So maybe they'll let you join us?"

"I doubt we'd be welcome," she replies. "Everyone's so crowded as it is."

"Are all the same people still in your carriage?"

"We've lost six."

"So maybe you can swap. I have a feeling Andreas would love to get away. There's an old man in our carriage who's constantly badgering him. Maybe someone else will want to move, too."

"We'd love to be with you. Shainie's been asking for you non-stop."

I hope the guards will allow us to switch. It means adjusting their lists, and they may not want to be bothered, but it's worth a try.

Because that's what it's about in the end. Not your house or your things or whether you're baking hot or whether there's an eye in the soup.

It's about holding on to one another when everything else slips away.

I take Shainie's hand and we wade in the cool blue water.

"Once upon a time …" I begin.

Author's Note

Dear Reader,

When I was in fifth grade, I always looked forward to Fridays because on Fridays our favorite teacher, Mr. Halpern, told us stories about his childhood. Amazing stories! Stories I never forgot.

A Boy Is Not a Bird is based on Nahum Halpern's own life story, starting in 1940, when the Russians occupied his town. That event marked the beginning of his long adventure. A photo from Nahum's childhood somehow managed to survive the war. There he is with his Hebrew-school classmates, standing next to his teacher, wearing his Scout uniform, when life was peaceful and happy.

In this book, I've given Nahum the name Natt Silver. The big life-changing events that take place really did happen as I describe them, but with Nahum's permission I've added conversations and everyday details, and I've also created characters based on historical figures who were around at the time.

But the story, we must never forget, is true.

A great teacher can change your life. Mr. Halpern's kindness, his sense of humor, love of teaching and uncanny understanding of children affected all his students. We loved him and tried to be model students for him. He inspired us to use our imagination, and he encouraged us to bring our unique personalities to bear on our learning.

Above all, he taught us the importance of being an honest, decent person throughout life, regardless of the hardships that might come our way. His philosophy never changed:

Be kind, do the right thing, consider others, and enjoy the funny and fantastic and weird things in life. Don't let anyone be an outsider. We all belong together.

May we all have a Mr. Halpern in our lives! I hope you enjoy his story. And if you have any questions or comments about his experiences, please send me a line ☺.

Yours,
Edeet (Dori)
aboyisnotabird@yahoo.com

PHOTO CREDIT: NAHUM HALPERN

Historical Background

Everyone knows the name of Adolf Hitler, the man who was determined to become dictator of Germany and eventually ruler of the entire world, and who was ready to crush anyone who got in his way.

As a young man, Hitler joined a group made up of "anti-Semites" — people who hated Jews and imagined that a secret Jewish group was running the world. The anti-Semites hoped to persuade everyone in Germany that Jews were to blame for all their problems.

Hitler still believed in these ideas when he became leader of the German state and then commander-in-chief of the army. Once his party — the Nazi Party — was in power, Jewish families were always going to be in danger.

Hitler kept saying that Germans needed *Lebensraum* — more space — when he really meant that he wanted more power. His plan to take over Europe began in March 1939, when he sent the German army marching into Czechoslovakia. Once that invasion was achieved, his next plan was to invade Poland. But he worried that Josef Stalin, the dictator of Russia (also known at that time as the Soviet Union or USSR), would send his armies to fight against a German invasion into neighboring Poland.

So Hitler suggested that the two of them sign a pact. Stalin agreed. The two leaders promised not to fight each other and decided who could take over which territories.

Secretly, Hitler never planned to keep his side of the deal. Sure enough, just two years later, his army swept deep into the Russian heartland, taking everyone there by surprise. There were huge numbers of casualties.

On both sides, this was a terrifying time for many ethnic minorities. Those who could not flee in time were in danger of losing their lives.

In Germany, the Nazis introduced a policy they secretly called the "Final Solution to the Jewish Question." Their "solution" was genocide — extermination camps with results that are too horrifying to comprehend.

And although a campaign of posters and propaganda depicted Stalin as a kind man, he, too, was a ruthless tyrant. He targeted Jews and other minorities, as well as "enemies of the people," a broad category that included ordinary citizens from every walk of life. He rounded up thousands of writers, scientists, priests, artists, actors, teachers, journalists, lawyers, doctors, university professors … the list is long.

How Natt Silver, the boy hero of this story, found his way through the many challenges thrown up by these big historical events is the subject of *A Boy Is Not a Bird* and the two volumes that will follow. The projected trilogy covers Natt's exile, his experiences in Siberia and his dramatic escape at the end of the war.

Acknowledgments

I am deeply grateful to those who have provided so much support and inspiration as I worked on this and other writing projects. I owe an enormous debt to:

Nahum Halpern, whose story this is, and who with characteristic generosity allowed me to transform it into a novel. I was extremely moved by the trust of Nahum and his wife, Gina, and their daughters, Tammy and Dafna.

The Groundwood team for believing in the book and making it happen with their usual impeccable flair, and to my editor there, Shelley Tanaka, to whom I owe special thanks for her insight, brilliant suggestions and ongoing enthusiasm. The late Sheila Barry is remembered by all who knew her for the love she brought to books and their creators; she is greatly missed. Semareh Al-Hillal's vote of confidence and warm encouragement have helped more than she knows.

Luke and Larissa, for being beautiful souls and for producing the astonishing Ivy.

Pam, who did the wonderful drawings for this book and whose friendship and talent and unfailing understanding have been a gift for three decades.

Ken Sparling, fellow writer who always gets it.

Richard Cooper, Reuben Shultz and John Detre for sharing historical/linguistic expertise and much more.

Joan Deitch, my London editor, long-time friend and confidante, prose magician, whose magnanimity knows no bounds.

Shirley Simha, who always listens (I'm amazed her ears have not fallen off by now).

And the many good friends whose kindness has made it all possible: Bob Symes, Chris and Jen Heap, Christianne Mann, Eve and Jose, Hope and Ken, Lil Blume, Lori and Marty, Margaret Wolfson, Mark Marshall, Terry Boyd and Joseph Dunlop-Addley and Marion Boyd, my brothers Uri and Uzi and sister Sara, Wonder Woman Wiebke Von Carolsfeld.

To the many other people who over the years have helped me release whatever good there was in me, I can only say, I am fortunate to have crossed your path.

The Canada Council for the Arts and the Ontario Arts Council provided financial assistance which enabled me to complete this book; I am extremely grateful to them both.

The excellent and unforgettable memoir for young readers, *The Endless Steppe: Growing Up in Siberia* by Esther Hautzig recounts the exile as it was experienced by a girl who was Nahum's contemporary. I consulted several other very moving memoirs, including *Sixteen Years in Siberia: Memoirs of Rachel and Israel Rachlin*; *Exiled to Siberia: A Polish Child's WWII Journey* by Klaus Hergt; *"Where the Devil Says Goodnight": Exile to Siberia, 1940-1946* by Alfreda Starza-Miniszewska, translated by Daniel Starza Smith, who kindly sent me the pages I requested; and "Romuald's Story: The Journey to Siberia" by Romuald Lipinski.

There are countless stories of exile, past and present. I hope we can hear them all.

Edeet (Dori) Ravel's young-adult novel *Held* was nominated for the CLA Young Adult Book Award and the Arthur Ellis Crime Award. Her young-adult novel *The Saver* has been adapted for film and received awards around the globe. Her acclaimed novels for adults have won the Hugh MacLennan Prize and the Jewish Book Award and have been nominated for the Governor General's Award and the Giller Prize.

Edeet was born on an Israeli kibbutz and holds a PhD in Jewish Studies from McGill University. She taught for twenty years at McGill, Concordia University and John Abbott College. She lives in Montreal.